Gaia's heart raced as she entered the building. She knew she was close. She could sense her father's presence. She entered the building and ran up the dank stairs. He was sure to be at the top; that was the most difficult place to escape from, because it could be seen from everywhere in the prison.

Rounding the last flight, she saw a cell at the end of a hallway. Inside it was a figure in a gray uniform, head bowed. It couldn't be so easy. But apparently it was. There, right before her eyes—

Don't miss any books in this thrilling series:

FEARLESS™

Available from SIMON PULSE

FEARLESS™

LUST

FRANCINE PASCAL

SIMON PULSE
New York   London   Toronto   Sydney   Singapore

First Simon Pulse edition September 2003

Copyright © 2003 by Francine Pascal

Cover copyright © 2003 by 17th Street Productions, an Alloy company.

SIMON PULSE
An imprint of Simon & Schuster Children's Publishing Division
1230 Avenue of the Americas, New York, NY 10020

Produced by 17th Street Productions,
an Alloy company
151 West 26th Street
New York, NY 10001

Fearless™ is a trademark of Francine Pascal.

Printed in the United States of America
10 9 8 7 6 5 4 3 2 1

Library of Congress Control Number: 2003106558
ISBN: 0-689-85766-7

To Colton and Gabrielle Bryan

I guess the only time most people think about blood is when it's gushing out of their veins and they need to find a Band-Aid—or an emergency room—to keep it from messing up the white carpet. But I've been thinking about it a lot lately. Little red platelets and big white corpuscles rushing through everyone's veins. Keeping us alive as long as it stays on its dark little course—but signaling weakness or death when it wanders off the path, out into the light to spill on the ground.

Funny thing about blood: It also connects people. There it is, hidden inside your skin, yet it manages to call out to other blood, related blood, inside someone else's skin. You might have nothing else in common, but that red stuff really is thicker than water. There's nobody in the world I should have more cause to hate than Oliver. Or should I say, Loki. He has engineered more destruction—starting with that of

my own mother, the woman who created the blood I'm talking about—
than anyone else in my life. So a
bout of postcoma confusion has
forced his pre-Loki, kinder and
gentler Oliver personality to
emerge, and suddenly he regrets
his evil ways.

At best I should feel indiffer-
ent toward him. But because we
share blood, I find myself drawn
to him. I find myself willing to
try to trust him—this new,
remorseful Oliver—because our DNA
matches up so nicely.

Am I just a sucker? A girl so
lonely she'll cling to any semblance of a family connection? Or
is this an instinct, speaking
through the bowels of primordial
history, telling me the tide has
turned for Oliver?

Let's hope it's the latter.

Let's hope it's the blood
that's letting me forgive him.
Anyone else would get nothing
from me but my everlasting hate.
Like Natasha and Tatiana, the
mother-daughter team from the

third ring of hell. A couple of
lying, conniving females who took
my dad from me and almost had me
convinced he was dead. But he
can't be dead. My blood would
tell me if he was. They're still
going to pay, though—maybe with
their own blood. If I get half a
chance, you can bet that'll be
the case.

But that's so a priority.
What's important now—what's got
to happen before anything else—is
I've got to find my dad. My real
blood link. Even closer than
Oliver. He's the one I owe my
loyalty to. And I'm going to find
him. Come hell or high water, the
blood pumping in my veins is
going to give me the strength to
reach around the globe and find
him. You can bet on that.

She had to

remember to

keep her

distance

unfamiliar

this

terrain

time.

Within her

heart, and

out in the

world.

Dangerously Accurate

GAIA SAT SLUMPED IN AN UNFORGIVING wood-and-metal chair as she cycled through the seven local stations one more time, looking for something that would amuse her and Jake in his hospital room. The television, which looked about twenty years old, was bolted to the ceiling and made a disconcerting fuzzy noise between each channel, like the *cchk* sound at the beginning and end of a walkie-talkie broadcast. The static was only marginally less interesting than daytime TV.

"Is this *Judge Judy*?" Gaia wanted to know.

"No, that's a different show" Jake said, pointing to the screen. "I forget what this one's called. . . . It looks like a judge show, but then they bring in therapists and it turns into a corny love fest where everybody's hugging and crying, even though tomorrow they're going to go back to throwing chairs at each other."

"Well, there's nothing else on. You need better health insurance. This no-cable thing is a problem."

"Aren't you supposed to be in school?" Jake asked again. Gaia glared at him.

"Didn't I already sidestep that question?" she wanted to know.

"Yeah, that's why I have to ask it again. I'd think

you'd be more considerate—it's tiring, ya know? All this verbal back-and-forth. . ."

"Whatever. I skipped again," she admitted. "I can't sit still in school. I'm too agitated."

"What? Because of this?" Jake shrugged. Gaia tried not to think about the fact that he'd been shot when he'd been ambushed. *Because* of her. So what if it had turned out to be nothing more than a flesh wound? He was hurt because he'd gotten in the way of people after Gaia. And that made her feel ill.

He wasn't the first person to end up lying on a metal cot with a tube in his arm because of her. And she felt a leaden certainty that he wouldn't be the last.

"Please. Don't flatter yourself," she said sheepishly, glancing at the bandages enveloping his powerful shoulder.

"Well, whatever it is, why don't you just go to school and avoid getting in trouble?"

Gaia blinked at him. "What are you, a Boy Scout?" she asked.

Jake laughed. "No, I'm just saying, you could go to school to pass the time just as easily as you can sit here."

Gaia knew he was right. She didn't know why she had such an aversion to school. Maybe it was because she already knew everything that was being droned about in the front of the classroom. Her dad—her dad and her mom, actually—had made sure of that, having made her take advantage of her sharp intellect from the moment she could read, which had happened at around age three. Maybe she just couldn't stand being fenced in. Maybe she was worried that another strike would hurt the students around her.

Or maybe she just wanted to be here, at the hospital, with Jake.

"Oh, why start behaving now?" she muttered. "It would just confuse everyone."

"You know what I think?" Jake gave her a sidelong look.

"No, in fact, I don't possess that particular skill," Gaia responded dryly.

"I think you like putting one over on people," he said with a tiny nod. "You like being Invisible Girl, appearing in class at will, while everyone else sticks to the rules and studies and worries about the SATs. Because you know you can pull a passing grade out of your ass, and you like the challenge."

"Oh, really?" Gaia knew she was just being teased. But even being fake-dissected gave her an uneasy feeling.

"Yeah. Plus, now that I know how crazy your life has been, it makes even more sense. You'd hate to feel settled and centered, wouldn't you? That would just be too unfamiliar to stand." Jake was enjoying this, Gaia could see that. She was acting nonchalant, but inside she squirmed with discomfort under the probing spotlight of this much attention. Not to mention the fact that his theory sounded dangerously accurate.

"Hey, I have a great idea, Jake. Why don't you get out of my head and back into your hospital bed? I think it's time for your lower G.I. series."

"Oh, hoooo!" Jake laughed at the sharp tone in Gaia's voice. "Man, are you easy to tease!"

"You're annoying," Gaia told him. "I'm going to request that your next sponge bath be given by a male nurse."

As if Gaia's guilty feelings had taken human form, the door clunked open and Jake's father entered the room, along with a stout old woman. Gaia stood up as if she'd been caught pulling the wings off a fly. She couldn't help but worry that Mr. Montone would eventually come to his senses and hold her responsible for Jake's condition. There was no way he could believe it was pure coincidence that his golden boy had gotten shot while he was out with his mysterious new friend.

"Gaia!" Mr. Montone came straight for her and gave her a. . . hug? Gaia's nerve endings did a confused little dance; they'd been expecting a slap, or at least the cold shoulder.

"It's so good to see you," Mr. Montone said. "You've been such a good friend to Jake through all this. Ma, this is Jake's friend Gaia. The one who got him to the hospital."

"You do so good!" the old woman said, reaching up to grab Gaia by the cheeks and giving her an affectionate—and powerful—squeeze.

"A lot of girls your age are somewhat. . . flighty," Mr. Montone added. "Might have panicked and run home. You really kept a level head, and I appreciate what you did for my son."

Gaia sent a telepathic thank you to the CIA agents who'd talked to Mr. Montone after the shootout. Who knew what on earth they could have told him? But whatever it had been, it had evidently completely ruled out any possibility of Gaia's involvement.

"Oh, no," Gaia stammered. "I mean, I didn't really—" *Shut up and quit while you're ahead*, she muttered internally. *For once, someone thinks you did something right. You'd better enjoy it.*

"Dad, Nonna, what are you guys doing here?" Jake asked. "Is something wrong?"

The door opened again. A nervous-looking young doctor in a white coat shuffled in, eyeballing the visitors who already seemed intent on bossing him around.

"Excuse me—I understand you want to take Jake home?" he asked, with all the authority of a kid who'd missed his curfew.

"We don' just wanna," Jake's grandmother said. "We *gonna* take him home."

The doctor looked to Jake's dad for help, but he just shrugged and started packing Jake's things into a duffel.

"Mrs. Montone, I really must tell you, we'd prefer it if we could watch Jake for one more night."

"Watch him what, starve to death because of your hospital food? I need to get some braciola into him before he fades to nothing."

Gaia snorted with laughter. She couldn't help it. Jake was so huge and solid that the idea of him wasting away was ridiculous.

"We'd just like to observe. . . oh. . . fine," the doctor said resignedly.

"Good man," Mr. Montone said, patting him on the back. "Don't worry, I can watch him. I know what to look for: infection, gangrene. I work at Mount Sinai, you know."

"Yes, sir."

It was amazing. Gaia hadn't noticed it as much back at Jake's apartment, but for all intents and purposes, Mr. Montone looked like an older Jake, only with white hair and a bit of a belly. He peered at Jake over his half-glasses and said, "You. Up."

"Gaia, do you mind?" Jake asked.

"What? Oh! I'll wait in the hall." She caught a glimpse of him sitting up and shifting over in bed, preparing to take off his hospital gown. Flustered, she left the room.

Immediately she realized she should have just made

her excuses and left. Of course, she could still just leave, but she hadn't said good-bye, and Jake's family would think she was weird.

And why do you care what Jake's family thinks? she asked herself.

I don't, she answered. *Who cares? Just because his father fed me the best homemade dinner I've had since I was a kid and welcomed me into his home, and just because his son is basically my only friend? I don't give a hoot what they think of me.* But somehow she stood in the hallway, shifting her weight from one foot to the other with nervous energy until they emerged.

Jake was fully clothed, except he hadn't managed to get a T-shirt over his bandages, so his loose flannel button-down shirt fell open at the chest. His dad and grandma followed behind him, arguing over which one should carry the duffel bag.

"Gimme that. You've got the bad back," his grandmother ordered.

"I've got it. It's not heavy," his dad said.

"Sure, it's-a not heavy till you throw your back out again. Come on, give."

Jake slowed down so that they had to pass him, then let the elevator door close without him.

"See you downstairs," he called out as his grandmother tried to hit the door-open button and failed.

"The hospital would have been some welcome peace and quiet," Jake said, indicating with a nod that he was referring to his father and grandmother.

"I think they're great," said Gaia.

"They are. But Nonna's a bit much." He sighed and hit the down button so they could get on the next elevator.

"Are you sure you should be going home?" Gaia asked.

"Oh, yeah," Jake said. "I fully expected my dad to show up and yank me out of here. He always says the best way to get sicker is to spend time in a hospital. This thing does ache, though."

"Yeek." Gaia peered at the big bandage. "I don't think you're going to be doing much intramural karate."

Jake groaned. "I know," he lamented. "You're off the hook, though. If I'm not competing, we won't win anyway."

"God, you've got the fattest head!" Gaia complained. "You think I couldn't beat everyone single-handedly?"

"You could, but you won't," he pointed out. "I was really looking forward to it, though. I was all revved up for the competition. Without it, the next few weeks are going to be so boring. And I'm going to get so out of shape."

Gaia felt the bud of an idea fatten in her head. "Hmm," she said.

"Hmm, what?" Jake asked, poking the button a few more times.

"Hmm, I was just thinking—when I was going

12

through my martial arts training, my dad showed me a bunch of techniques for working out that give various muscle groups a rest. I could teach them to you, just so your precious muscle mass doesn't evaporate during your recovery."

Gaia couldn't believe the words that were coming out of her mouth. Was she actually being forthcoming? This Jake guy had a very unusual effect on her.

"Gaia Moore, are you offering to be my personal trainer?"

She rolled her eyes. "Yeah, right. If you're going to be an idiot about it, I won't bother."

Jake smacked her lightly on the back of the head. "Cut it out," he said. "I'm sorry. I would be really grateful if you could show me your special commando workout."

"Fine. I will," Gaia said.

"But only if you go to school tomorrow."

"Fine."

"Of course, you're going to be gone within a day or two," Jake pointed out as the elevator finally arrived and the doors creaked open. "Some 911 situation will come up and you'll be out of here. I'll be left with atrophying muscles and a gunshot wound."

For a moment, Gaia had a vision of Sam Moon's scarred chest—another wounded friend, a romance destroyed by the life she was forced to lead. She had to

13

remember to keep her distance this time. She wouldn't let the same thing happen to Jake.

Gaia was silent, watching the numbers light up in descending order. This was the slowest elevator in the world. She noticed Jake giving her a look.

"What?" she snapped.

"I think it's funny," he said.

"*What*?"

"The way every single thought in your head goes walking across your face before you shove it back in its closet," Jake said. "You really think that because you don't say things out loud, you can deny they're there, don't you?"

"All right, smart guy—so what thoughts am I repressing?" she asked, crossing her arms and continuing to stare as nine flipped to eight with agonizing sluggishness.

"Oh, no. I'm not making things easier for you. You'll open your mouth when you're good and ready, and not before."

Gaia clamped her mouth tightly closed, tucking her lips inside it for extra emphasis, and refused to look at Jake. He was so close to her, she could feel the heat from his body making the left side of her face flush. Without her permission, her eyes flicked toward him, then away again. The expression in his eyes—he seemed to *know* her in a way she wasn't sure was either good or bad. He was teasing her, daring her to feel something for him. It was maddening, frustrating.

The doors finally opened. "Jake!" Mrs. Montone called out, her arms extended as if she were about to reach in and yank him out. "Why you sneak off like that? Come here."

Jake shot Gaia one last look and joined his father and grandmother, who draped a coat carefully over his shoulders.

"Gaia, can you get home all right?" Mr. Montone asked. "Should we drop you somewhere? We've got a car service waiting."

"Oh, no, it's all right," Gaia promised. "I can take the subway."

"Are you sure? It's no trouble."

Gaia was touched. If Mr. Montone knew what she'd been through in her life, the guy wouldn't have been concerned about her being inconvenienced by the midday subway.

"I promise. It was nice to see you again. And nice to meet you, Mrs. Montone."

"Yeah, I see you again," she said, nodding cheerfully.

"So I'll see you tomorrow after school?" Jake asked. "You'll show me that stuff we were talking about?"

Gaia felt herself nod. Maddening, yes. Frustrating, yes. But whether it was out of guilt or some kind of unexpected fascination, she'd have to see Jake again.

OLIVER SEARCHED THROUGH THE databases he had found stored on his computer—the ones that hadn't self-destructed when he'd gotten his log-in wrong the first time. It had taken him half a day just to get access to his own information. This was like trying to put together one of those all-black jigsaw puzzles. In the dark. During a windstorm. If something looked familiar, he had to then ask

Internal Hard Drive

himself why, and what it might connect to, and how he should approach it. He felt like a blind man in a maelstrom.

Finding this information required the highest level of mental functioning. For someone so recently out of a coma, it was exhausting. And there was something else that was required: To access some of the memories he needed—passwords, log-in names, locations of files, meanings of notes—he had to force some of Loki's memories to the surface. And Oliver was not a computer; he couldn't just pull up one file out of a folder and leave the rest safely closed. If he exposed one memory to the light, others would try to bubble to the surface as well. And he could not afford to have that happen.

He was dancing a dangerous tango with his evil former self.

Oliver took a long drink of water and turned his eyes to the screen again. He had to secure transportation for them. Airline tickets. How did this work again? He had to get the passports in another name, the visas to match, enough tickets for everyone. . . . The screen began to swim in front of him. It seemed to morph into a television screen. On it he saw a man—a man dressed as a doctor—in an antiseptic room, a white room, but not a hospital. A loft of some kind. . . A young woman was there, a girl, a friend of Gaia's; something in him told him that. The scene was new but dripping with familiarity, like in dreams where some subconscious voice acts as a narrator for unfamiliar terrain.

The girl bent over and the doctor injected her with something. Oliver squinted to see more clearly. Then the screen split; on one side, he saw the beautiful young woman struck blind as a result of the injection. On the other side he saw the doctor raise his face. With horror, Oliver recognized his own eyes staring back at him from the television screen.

Jolted, he jumped back, knocking his chair to the floor with a clatter. The noise made him look down, and when he looked back up, the taunting television screen had become his computer again—his safe, familiar computer, quietly listing his old contacts for him to pore over.

"Loki," he said out loud. "It was Loki, and I have control over him."

He straightened the chair and placed it in front of his desk again, glanced nervously at the computer screen. But it was still covered in calm, static numbers. No more streaming video straight from his buried internal hard drive. Oliver took a deep breath and sat down again.

He needed to find a few contacts who would still do him favors. He needed to check those favors, to be sure he was not being scammed. He had to secure these passports and visas. His brother's life depended on it. Gaia's happiness depended on it.

He mustered his energy and forced himself back to work.

"WELL, LOOK, WE'VE INTERVIEWED A bunch of guys, but you're the only one who seems normal. If you want the place, it's yours."

Outer-Borough Frat House

Sam Moon took the hand extended to him and shook it. "That's great, man," he said. "I appreciate it. You want the check now?"

"Yeah, if you've got it."

Sam nodded and went into the room that was going to be his. The two guys—his new roommates—who already lived here seemed cool. They were students, but not at NYU, so Sam didn't have to worry that they'd know of his strange past.

This room—something about an empty room made it full of possibilities. The wide wooden slats of the floor invited him to plop a futon down. The cavernous closet, with nothing but two wire hangers and a baseball cap inside, awaited his meager wardrobe. The pale walls, painted an indiscriminate shade of greige, were made for dorm-style décor—black-and-white art posters, an Escher print, maybe an Anna Kournikova calendar. It was like a blank canvas.

He strolled to the windows and looked out. The windows were old and heavy. They rolled up and down on thick chains, and he could feel a palpable breeze where the frames met the jambs. They looked out on a busy Queens boulevard, filled with at least six different international restaurants, based on a quick count. Afghan, Indian, Chinese, Mexican, Greek, and something in a language he didn't even recognize. So he didn't live in Manhattan anymore. So he was going to have to work for a while before he could get back to school. That was okay. Because he finally had some kind of control over his life.

Of course he was worried. Of course he knew he could still be a target. But living in hiding, in Chinatown with Dmitri, was no longer an option. He couldn't live like a caged animal anymore. Dmitri was great—it was a loan from him that was making this all possible, after all—but he was just one more reminder of that whole bizarre Gaia chapter of his life.

Gaia. She was the most fantastic, sexy, romantic, exciting person he'd ever known, but being with her had come with a price. Whatever mysterious forces she was connected to had destroyed Sam's life. Operatives bent on destroying Gaia had come after him, killing his roommate, framing him for the murder, and finally shooting and imprisoning Sam for months. He still wasn't fully recovered, physically or mentally. And Gaia hadn't come through for him. Yeah, she had rescued him, but when he'd tried to reconnect with her, she'd thrown up so many walls that he just hadn't been able to. Plus there was that boyfriend of hers. Obviously she was still stuck on him. There just wasn't room in her heart for Sam Moon.

That had been painful. So rather than be halfway in her life, he'd made the decision to cut himself off from her entirely. Make a fresh start. Hence the empty room in this outer-borough frat house.

Yeah, he was taking a chance. Whoever had hurt him the first time could be after him still. But he was as good as dead, hidden away in Dmitri's apartment. He had to take this chance.

"Dude, you okay in there? We were just going to get

some beers—you want to come with?"

"Yeah! I was just looking for my checkbook," Sam said, scribbling out a check for a ridiculous amount of money and taking it out to the living room. "Here you go. First and last month's rent, plus a security deposit."

The beers were going to cost Sam pretty much everything left in his account, but that was okay with him. Pretty much everything was okay with him right now. He was completely psyched to restart his life. All he had to do now was find a job.

So what could a guy with a back full of scar tissue and half a college education do to pull down some cash?

He followed his new friends to the dark Irish pub downstairs and watched three beers get ripped open in rapid succession. He took one and tipped it back, feeling the cool bubbles slip down his throat. Of course. Why hadn't he thought of it before? He had enough hard-luck stories of his own to know how to listen to everyone else's. He'd be a bartender.

I see mountains. Snowy mountains. They're beautiful, cold, remote. I'm not a fool. I recognize them. I am in Siberia.

Siberia. Like some kind of Soviet Union-era dissident. I suppose it has its own romantic appeal. Except, of course, that most of those dissidents ended up dying of consumption.

I'm amazed at how calm I'm remaining. I know that I'm infuriated enough to bang my head against the wall of my jail cell, to grab the bars of my cell and pull on them until my knuckles break. This is unbearable.

I'm in Siberia, a region so remote it doesn't even have regular telephones, let alone cell phones.

My cell is eight by eight. Too small for a primate at the Bronx Zoo.

I can see the other prisoners exercising in the courtyard. I'm not even allowed to socialize with them. I'm locked up here like Hannibal Lecter.

And who's to blame for all this?

Loki. Once again, Loki.

The human mind cannot bear this kind of cruelty. Mere days ago, I was in the arms of my soon-to-be wife, enjoying the rosy glow of my new family. Watching Gaia become close to her new stepsister, Tatiana. Eyeballing Gaia's boyfriend, Ed. What made me think I could be a normal father with a normal family? What made me consider the idea of taking Ed aside to make sure he had Gaia's best interests at heart? I'm no father. I couldn't even stay clear of the evil creature who was once my brother long enough to finish dinner. Before it was done, I remember coughing. . . then choking. . . then blackness. Until I woke up here.

He did it to me again.

Perhaps my calm comes from the knowledge that this time I will destroy him. This time I will make Loki pay for the pain he has caused me, by eradicating him from the earth altogether. No matter what.

Even if it costs me my own life.

A week ago
she'd been
wishing
Oliver dead—
now she was
bantering
over
cell phone
etiquette
with him.

the old psycho—killer

"OW. OKAY, THAT HURTS."

Dripping With Nostalgia

"It's supposed to."

"Yeah, but it really hurts."

"No pain, no gain, Jake."

"No gain, then! *Ack!*" Jake dropped the bulbous kettle-drum he had been holding up with his foot. It hit the floor with a crash, which was immediately followed by three thudding sounds from the floor below.

"That's old lady Teverasky," Jake said. "I think you made her week. She loves hitting her ceiling with her broomstick—it reminds her of the old country, where they do that for sport."

"Don't try to distract me," Gaia said, crossing her arms. "I'm supposed to be keeping you in shape."

"What shape? A rectangle?" Jake flopped backward on the couch.

"A rectangle? Why a rectangle?"

"Because that's what I feel like: a wreck and a tangle." He looked up at Gaia, who was trying to be really firm and drill-sergeanty.

"That's it, I give up," she said, flopping down next to him on the couch. "Your bad jokes are draining me."

"Oh, good, I give up, too," Jake said.

"You know, you're not going to get any stronger if you don't keep working out," she scolded him.

25

"You know what? Forget it," he said. "I've been on a workout regimen since I was, like, twelve years old. I think a couple of weeks off is just what I need."

"Whatever. Just don't come crying to me when you wake up and realize you're Mister Flabby."

"And what'll you be, Miss Crabby?"

Gaia snorted. Actually, that stung a little. She knew she was hard to get along with. Lord knew she'd lost enough friends along the way—more than most people made in a lifetime. She wasn't sure—she was never sure—if Jake was just kidding. So far, he always was. But she'd seen Ed, good old best-friend-cum-boyfriend Ed, go from being an easy-going buddy to being a jaded, bitter ex in no time flat.

She had to admit, though, that being with Jake felt nice. Mellow, sort of.

"So are you still feeling. . . agitated?" he asked cautiously. Gaia suddenly felt the walls closing in on her.

"I don't want to talk about it," she said, standing up and walking to the window. She felt bad for snapping at him, but she had to be careful about telling him too much. At the same time, she knew that her evasiveness made her seem ungrateful.

"Hey, okay, we won't," he said, trying to play it off. "You don't have to tell me anything you don't want to," Jake said. "I was just asking so I wouldn't be a dick for not asking."

That evoked a small smile. "I know, Jake. I didn't mean to snap at you."

She turned back and looked at him. "I have to go to Urban Outfitters to get new sneakers," she said. "I've been putting it off, but when my old ones got melted—well, just look at them." She held up one foot and displayed the way her ancient Chuck Taylor sneaker had split where the rubber met the fabric. Her sock poked out of the hole, and the sole was a mushed-up, melted mess.

"Nice," Jake said. "But weren't you caught in that fire like a week ago?"

"Something like that. I'm having separation anxiety. I've had these sneakers forever."

"It's time to let them rest in peace," Jake said somberly. "They've done their job. They're tired."

"Want to come with?" she asked.

"Nah. I'm tired. I'm going to take full advantage of my gimpy state and rest up a little."

Gaia knew Jake's shoulder was still bothering him from the shooting. She also knew better than to ask him about it. He was as private as she was—another thing she liked about him. "All right, I'll see you later," she said. "Don't get up. I'll let myself out."

"I wasn't getting up," Jake called after her. Gaia gave him a smirk as she went through the door.

Urban Outfitters was on lower Broadway. The walk wasn't long, but Gaia's poor old sneakers kept ripping, so by the time she got inside they were like flip-flops.

27

Gaia strolled around the shoe section, immediately rejecting the sneakers that had sparkles or platform soles. All she wanted was to grab a pair of Chuck Taylors identical to the ones ruined in the fire and get out of the cavernous store. But they were nowhere to be found.

"Chuck Taylors?" she asked the nearest salesperson.

"Uh, yeah, maybe if you visited the time-machine section of our store," she said snottily. "Try the Pumas, I guess."

Gaia tried on a pair of the black suede sneakers, marveling at how big her feet were. They felt like two little comfortable homes. She eyeballed her old Chucks, sitting forlornly next to her spanking-new shoes.

"Sorry, guys," she told them. "It was great while it lasted, but we should have parted ways long ago."

Gaia strolled up the sidewalk at her usual rapid pace. Lower Broadway was jammed with people, as usual, and she was bumping through them, heading uptown, when one bumped her especially hard, knocking her backward slightly.

"Oof! Watch where you're—Sam!"

She had literally bumped into Sam Moon. She hadn't seen him since their final, melancholy conversation. The one where Sam had basically told her that even though they were practically soul mates who had been though hell together, he just couldn't deal with her weird, shut-down personality and never wanted to see her again. Sam, the guy who'd been the first to pitch his flag on the surface of her heart. Gaia looked up at him, seeing the uncertainty and discomfort on his face.

"Hey," he said. He didn't exactly look happy to see her. Then again, he didn't look unhappy, either.

"What are you up to?" Gaia asked.

"I had to come here to get my new uniform," he admitted, in a sheepish tone that made Gaia feel protective of him. "I'm working at a restaurant. As a bus boy, for now. But they say I can work my way up eventually."

"Oh, man, that's great," Gaia told him, but inside, her heart sank a bit.

"Well, not really," Sam admitted. "I walked in there thinking I was going to be a bartender. Do you know they actually ask for resumes now?"

"Did you tell them you were a premed at NYU?" Gaia asked. "I mean, if you can pass organic chemistry, I'm sure you can mix a cosmopolitan."

"I don't think they see it that way."

"So where are you working? Is it somewhere near Dmitri's?"

"I actually. . ." Sam looked down, as though he couldn't really stand to meet Gaia's gaze. Then he took a breath. "I don't want to tell you where I'm working," he blurted out. "And I'm not living with Dmitri anymore."

"Oh." Gaia didn't know what to say. For once she didn't have a wisecrack or a comeback.

"I just needed a change," he went on. "I—this whole thing, it's just too strange. I need to make a complete break."

"Okay."

"It's nothing personal. I thought we could remain friends, but. . ." He shrugged.

"No, that's cool. You need space," Gaia said. "Time to get used to the outside world. I think I know how that goes." *Besides*, she thought, *I've sworn off friends for good, so it wouldn't work out anyway.*

"Yeah, I guess." He still couldn't quite look at her. They were so near the NYU dorm where he'd lived when they were dating. The whole scene was `dripping with nostalgia.`

"Don't lose my phone number, okay?" Gaia pleaded. "You never know when you might need someone to talk to. Someone who knows what you went through."

"Uh-huh." Sam was turning into Mister One-Syllable. This was too strange, too different from the Sam she used to know. Gaia wanted to get away.

"I won't be isolated," he said finally. "I've got roommates and everything. And there's the job," he added, waving his black pants and white shirt halfheartedly.

"I'm sure you'll be a bartender in no time," Gaia said, trying to sound reassuring. "Or even maître d'.

Can you speak with a French acc-*sant*? Maybe grow a little pencil moustache?"

"I'll think about it." Sam finally looked at her, and Gaia felt a little wiggle in her heart.

"I'm really happy you're making a clean break," she told him. "I think this'll be good."

"Thanks. Well. So I'm gonna go," he said, giving her a small wave.

Gaia waved back and walked away. Then she realized she was walking the complete opposite direction of where she needed to go. She'd have to take a different train now, from the west side, and go crosstown on the shuttle. But that was infinitely more attractive than running into Sam again and repeating the awkward scene she'd just been through.

Seeing Sam could not have been more uncomfortable. They'd been completely in love not that long ago, and now he was like a total stranger. Worse than that—he was like an *acquaintance*, someone she barely knew and didn't care about. But she did care about him. She cared about him, but she was mad at him, sort of, for not understanding her better. And she was mad at herself—furious, in fact—for being the reason he was feeling so screwed up. If he'd never met her—if he had just kept dating Heather—well, they'd both have been okay. He wouldn't have been shot, and Heather wouldn't have been struck blind, and everything would have been hunky-dory. The only ruckus

31

would have been Heather's search for a dress to wear to his winter formal. But because of her, because of Gaia Moore, they were both in their own total messes.

And then there was Ed. Ed had been her best friend. She could hang out with him from morning till night and never get sick of him. They could be silent together, or they could talk about nothing and everything. Then they'd started dating, and everything in Gaia's life had seemed to blow up at once. She'd seen Ed threatened. And she'd also gotten distracted. In the end, Ed had gotten hurt, too. Not physically, but hurt just the same—badly. And he seemed to absolutely hate her now.

And finally there was Jake, who she hadn't even gotten close to yet, but who had already been shot. What else did she want?

She had to cross through Washington Square Park to get to the train. There weren't many people around at this time of day. The late afternoon shadows slanted long across the concrete tiles, and an eerie silence hung over the park. Gaia tried to shake off a feeling that something was about to happen, but some kind of spider-sense prickled within her. This time of day was always a little spooky, but she did hear something—a struggle. Somebody fighting, being shushed, being told to keep quiet while somebody else. . .

Gaia sprang into action. The sound was coming from the bushes by the gross little concrete buildings that passed as public restrooms. As she raced toward them, she could see a man and a woman locked in some kind of scuffle. The woman was much smaller than the man; Gaia could see her thin white arms flailing at her sides.

Gaia leapt in the air and knocked the man straight to the ground. He was concentrating so hard on mugging his victim that she took him completely by surprise. He offered no resistance as she fell on top of him.

"Take off, punk!" she demanded, but the guy wouldn't leave. He seemed to be trying to reach for the woman, even now. God, what a persistent little pervert he was.

"Ohmigod! Ohmigod, Rob, *help*! We're being mugged!"

"Just run," Gaia told her, not stopping to ask why she'd said "we," when clearly she was the only one getting mugged.

"Don't touch me!" the woman screamed, reaching into her purse. Gaia turned to tell her more firmly to stop panicking and run her ass out of the park, when she felt her eyes explode with pain.

"*Agh!* Did you *mace* me?" she asked.

"Rob, come on, quick," the woman shrieked, and Rob—the mugger—got up and followed her, while Gaia staggered a few steps away. She could hear them talking to a policeman almost immediately.

"We were in the park, and this wild woman attacked us!" The woman was still shrieking.

"Where were you, exactly?" the officer wanted to know.

"Well, we were. . . standing by the public restroom," the woman said.

"*Standing?*" the officer asked suspiciously.

"Okay, more like standing and kissing. . . Maybe we got a little carried away with each other," the guy said.

"I sprayed her with my pepper spray!" the woman added proudly.

Oh. *Oh, crap.* Gaia had a feeling the cop wouldn't be in too big a hurry to find her, but she didn't want to wait to find out. Her eyes still burned, and she was sure they were bright red and puffy. And she was horribly, horribly embarrassed.

What was the matter with her? She couldn't tell the difference between a horny couple and a mugging in progress? Had she lost all common sense?

No, she'd just misread her instincts because she was distracted—again. The frustration of running into Sam had thrown her off. And she'd taken it out on this guy Rob.

She got to the subway and descended the stairs, blinking painfully. She felt so stupid. Worse than stupid—she felt like a total and complete asshole.

What was that Bob Marley song? Who the cap fit, let them wear it.

She *was* an asshole.

"YOU ASSHOLE!" KAI LAUGHED. SHE

Complete Lack of Drama

tried to shoot Ed Fargo back, but her laser gun was disabled for fifteen seconds because he'd gotten her smack in the back. He took this chance to escape through a back alley into the main room.

That was when the kid got him.

He couldn't have been more than eight years old, but he was quick, and Ed suspected he had a little-kid crush on Kai. He couldn't blame the little guy. Kai was like a Japanese anime character come to life: baggy pants, half-shirt, pigtails, and a thousand-watt smile. Plus she had enough energy to light Manhattan. She was a great girl, tons of fun, and Ed was fully enjoying spending time with her. Which was why the kid must have decided to fry Ed.

Pa-tchoo!

The pack on Ed's chest made a *wee-wee-wee* noise and Ed was completely disabled. Kai could walk up to him and shoot his bull's-eye as much as she wanted, which was what she did. Knowing their ten minutes in the laser room were almost up, he let his arms flop to his sides and just surrendered. Right on cue, the buzzer signaled the end of the session.

"You got me," he admitted. "You win. But next time, no fair enlisting munchkins to help you."

"I'm not a munchkin," the kid said.

"No, you're my hero," Kai told him, and ruffled his hair. The kid gave Ed the finger and raced off to find his parents.

"What the—" Ed pulled off his laser backpack and strolled with Kai to the front entrance. "These kids today—I'm telling you, they've got no respect."

"Yeah," Kai responded.

"Want to go get some really cheap Chinese food? There's a place on Ninth Avenue that's got the biggest combination plate you ever saw."

"Sure! That's cool!"

Sure! That's cool! Ed savored the words as they danced around in his head. No sarcastic comments, no pointed references, no distractions or family emergencies or mysterious chokings. Just Kai. Ed reached over and took her hand, and she squeezed his back enthusiastically.

"So that was fun when we went to Chelsea Piers to go rock-climbing," he said.

"Totally!"

"And I didn't realize that crazy boat ride at the South Street Seaport was so high-octane."

"I know!"

"So what are we going to do next?"

"I've got a plan in the works. A friend of my dad's

works at a construction site, and I think he'll let us go up in one of his cranes."

"Agh!" Ed yelped. "Do you really want to do that?"

"Why not?" Kai shrugged. "If all those construction guys can do it, I'm sure we can. You're not scared of heights, are you?

No, but. . . oh what the hell, Ed thought. Kai was such a breath of fresh air, he'd pretty much follow her into the gates of hell at this point. After all the petty bitchery of Heather, the frustration of Gaia, the multiple-personality disorder of Tatiana, he was having the time of his life. And Kai seemed seriously into him.

Finally, he had figured out what he wanted from a woman. Fun, fun, and a complete lack of drama.

You hear that, Gaia? A complete lack of drama!

A Good Anecdote

GAIA DIDN'T WANT TO GO HOME after all. Her run-in with Sam had rattled her, and her mistake in the park hadn't helped. Instead, she pulled out her cell phone and dialed Oliver's number.

"Gaia," he said, startling her.

"I hate that you have caller ID,"

she told him, laughing a little. "I've got to remember to block my number so you can't do that to me."

"Sorry. I'll play dumb when you call."

She was struck silent for a moment. A week ago she'd been wishing Oliver dead—now she was bantering over cell phone etiquette with him.

"I suppose you would have called if any of the deliveries had arrived," she said.

"That's true."

"So there's been no change?"

"I'm sorry, Gaia, there's been no change. I'm working on it."

"I know." She kicked the concrete curb. "Do you know when?

"It could be in an hour, it could be next week," he said. "The wheels are in motion, and I'm keeping in contact with everyone. But it's a touchy situation. I don't have many friends left, it seems."

"It'll be okay," Gaia told him, then hung up the phone. Just as she had so many times these last few days, she found herself feeling sorry for the old psycho-killer.

This was frustrating. She had to stay off Oliver's back and let him do his job. But she was bored. School was out for the day, she'd already been to Jake's, and . . . well, she didn't have any other friends, not anymore. The afternoon and evening stretched out in front of her like. . . like a really long afternoon and evening. She was so bored, even clever metaphors escaped her.

Saved by the bell, she thought as her phone chirped. It was Jake. Gaia hated to admit how glad she was.

"Yeah?" she asked.

"I'm bored," he said.

"I thought you were tired."

"I *was* tired. Of working out. Now I'm bored and I'm going to go to the comic book store. You coming?"

"Yeah, but it might take a while. I have to take a roundabout route to the east side."

"What? Why?"

"Long, long story. I beat up the wrong person."

Jake laughed long and hard in her ear. Gaia grimaced.

"Do you mind?" she asked. "It's not that funny."

"Actually, it is," he told her. "See you when we get there."

Gaia hung up. This was humiliating. But when she thought about it, she realized that maybe it was sort of funny. Some day Attack of the Killer Kiss-Monster would make a good anecdote.

Was that a bad idea? I'm supposed to play it cool with girls,
not spend all my time with them
when they pique my interest. But
I *am* bored, and even though she
just left my apartment, I want to
see Gaia again. I'm not going to
play some stupid keep-my-distance
game just to prove something to
my testicles. Besides, she's
about to leave town to go on some
mysterious mission. If I stick to
the Cool Rule, I might not see
her at all before she goes. Then
I'd feel like a total idiot.

What the hell.

Anyway, Gaia's not a girl per
se. I mean, she is, but not like
any girl I've met before. She's
not into shopping, she's not into
gossip, but she's also not so
punk rock that she hates all
girlie things just to make a
statement. She seems to be above
it all—I mean, just outside of
everything that most kids in high
school think is dementedly important. It's like she's lived more

than she's supposed to already.
She's seen more of the world than
she has a right to at her age.
And something about that—I just
want to be near it. I want to
soak it up.

So she won't be my prom date. I
can't picture her in a dress,
anyway. But girls like that are a
dime a dozen. Gaia's mysterious.
She's got so much going on. She's
on a whole different level.

I had no idea, when I found out
I was switching schools, that I'd
find such a prize. It's like I'm
getting a taste of the real
world. And I just want more.

"TRY IT ON."

"I'm not trying it on."

"Come on, just the hood."

"The hood is the worst part."

"The cape, then."

"Jake, you're going to have to fulfill your fantasies some other way. I am not putting on that ridiculous getup."

Feeling of Foreboding

"I'm going to have to ask you to put that down," the salesclerk said. Gaia was quick to oblige. Jake, on the other hand, was clearly offended by the clerk's request.

"Let's get out of here—I want to get some dinner, anyway," Gaia said, defusing any potential "situation." "C'mon, I'll buy you some rice and beans."

"That's a whole dollar fifty," Jake called after her as she strode out of the store. "I can't let you do that."

They went to Burritoville around the corner and ordered. But just as they were digging into their Mexican concoctions, Gaia's phone bleated.

"This has to be good news," she said. "Unless it's a wrong number."

But it wasn't a wrong number. It was Oliver. Gaia made a few grunts of agreement, then snapped her phone shut. Her eyes were shining as she turned back to Jake.

"I've got to go."

"But your food," Jake said, knowing it sounded

lame, but not quite ready to watch her walk away for a week—or for the rest of his life.

"I'm not hungry anymore. I gotta go."

"Let me come with you."

Gaia turned to him, her forehead wrinkling. "What, are you kidding me?"

"You may as well let me. I'm just going to follow you, anyway."

"Yeah, right. I could lose you in half a second."

Jake gave a frustrated sigh. "Just let me come with you."

"Jake, this has nothing to do with you!"

"I've got bullet holes in my arm that beg to differ." The veins in Jake's forehead were bulging. "I mean, the least you could do to show your gratitude is to condescend to let me follow you."

That shut Gaia right up. Her eyes narrowed. "I guess it's okay," she said, shrugging. "But we have to go all the way out to Brooklyn."

"That's cool."

"Just. . . be careful, okay?"

Jake followed Gaia up Third Avenue, toward the L train. Oliver lived on that line, past the hipster part of Williamsburg and deep in the no-man's-land of Greenpoint.

But as soon as they got on the train, Jake sensed something was wrong. He looked at Gaia, but she was hard to read. She seemed deep in concentration. He supposed he was just imagining things. Still, his uneasy feelings hovered like a cloud over his head as they passed stop after stop. The other people on the train seemed innocent enough. So why this feeling of foreboding?

Finally Gaia stirred as they pulled into a station. "Come on," she said in a low voice. "Stay close to me. Someone's been casing us."

"I knew it," Jake muttered. "Who?"

"The cop. He's not a real cop. The badge is fake."

Jake was astounded. He hadn't noticed that. The cop would have been the last person he'd have suspected. Sure enough, when they got off the train, the police officer followed them. He didn't say a word, just tailed them up the steps to the street, where the sky was darkening and the air was purple with dusk. Three other men stepped out of the shadows and stood around them, ranged like numbers on a clock face.

They came closer. Alarms went off in Jake's head.

It was go time.

He'd known
better than
to expect
St. John's
or Montego
Bay to have
any place on
Gaia Moore's
travel
itinerary.

hello
kitty
clips

GAIA STEPPED BACK A PACE, AND

Fake Cop

Jake instinctively turned his back to her. If they were going to be surrounded, they could at least guard their perimeter completely. He crouched slightly, ready to fight. Then he listened, tuning to Gaia, letting her take the lead.

The moment Jake was in a fighting stance, Gaia struck. One of their attackers came too close and caught a foot in his gut. At the same time, she sent whirling fists to the other guy on her side, and Jake did his best to keep up his end of the fight. The pain in his shoulder felt like a tearing of muscle from bone, but he couldn't worry about that. Running on pure adrenaline, he mustered up all his fighting skills, combining every martial art he'd ever studied to confront the fists coming his way. He pulled the first guy toward him, using his momentum to yank him to the ground and stomp him with a kick to the head. That took care of him for the moment, anyway.

He couldn't see Gaia anymore; things were happening too fast. The "cop" was next, and to Jake's horror—especially since he now knew what a bullet wound felt like—he saw him draw the NYPD-issue pistol from its holster. He thought of Indiana Jones shooting the sword-fighter and threw himself headlong at the guy's waist, hoping he'd get there before the gun could be cocked and fired.

Somehow, he did. The guy had the flabby paunch of a cop, that was for sure—that was probably why he'd been so convincing—and Jake hit it full force, causing the guy to stumble backward. He heard the gun drop to the ground and kicked it, soccer-style, halfway down the block.

He turned and saw an amazing sight: Gaia was fully whipping the other *three* guys, all at the same time. It was like something out of a movie. Every time one got up, another seemed to fall so that she could keep fighting. He tried to join in, but wasn't sure where he'd fit. The fake cop stood up and Jake flattened him with a two-fisted punch that knocked his head against the hard wall of a brownstone. It was a lucky shot. Gaia kicked another assailant down the subway steps and turned to him.

"This is the best we're going to be able to do for now," she said. "Can you run?"

"If I have to," he told her. "I'd rather finish these guys off."

"No way. No time. This is good enough for now. Come on," she said in a hoarse staccato, and took off.

Jake had never seen anything like this. She ran like a wild animal, like she was in fast motion; it was all he could do to keep her in sight. Their attackers didn't seem to be behind him—he heard them start to give chase, but they soon stopped. Just to be safe, Gaia led them around a few extra turns, taking a long route to Oliver's brownstone. When they arrived, she buzzed frantically, leaning on the door till it opened; Jake followed and they both dropped to the floor in the foyer, waiting.

Nothing. No pounding footsteps following them up the steps. No smash as the glass of the door was broken. No innocent-sounding buzz from their assailants, hoping to gain access without attracting attention. There was nothing.

"Who the hell were they?" Jake wanted to know.

"Some men who don't want me to—," Gaia answered. But her voice dropped off. Jake turned, his face grazing the grimy black-and-white tiles of the floor, to see Gaia's eyes rolling back in her head as she blacked out.

"Gaia?" he said. "Did something happen? Did you get hit? Gaia!"

A door at the top of the stairway opened and Oliver came out.

"Something happened to Gaia," Jake said, frantic now. "She passed out or something. These guys attacked us, and—"

"It's all right," Oliver said, moving quickly but calmly down the stairs. "Come on, help me get her inside. This is what happens to her after a fight. Using all that strength saps her energy."

This was getting stranger and stranger. Jake grabbed Gaia's legs and helped carry her up the dingy staircase. "I'm not exactly full of energy myself," he admitted, feeling his shoulder start to ache painfully.

"Different for her," Oliver huffed. "Superstrength. Supertired." They plopped her gently on the couch and Oliver turned to Jake.

"I'm glad you were with her," he said.

"Do you know who those guys were?"

Oliver ignored Jake's question. "We need to go now."

Jake nodded. "I guess you do."

Oliver gave him a strange look, like he was afraid to say what was on his mind.

"What?" Jake asked.

"They've seen you," Oliver said. "Not once, but twice. They know who you are. It's unsafe for you here. Especially now that Gaia and I are leaving."

Something shifted in Jake. Some sense of inevitability dawned on him. Before, he'd sort of been flirting with the idea of getting involved in something larger than his own life, something mysterious and dangerous. Now it was as if he'd wandered too long in the jungle and couldn't get out.

"You mean I can't just walk away," Jake said. It wasn't really a question. It was more a statement of something he already understood.

Oliver shook his head slowly. "I don't think so," he said.

"What do I do?" Jake asked. He thought of going home, then imagined what would happen there if he were tailed by people like the fake cops from the L train. His dad. His grandma. He suddenly felt a wave of homesickness that was more about sickness than home. "I can't go back, can I?"

Oliver looked at him with a cool, steady gaze. "It would be best to lay low for a while," he said.

"What about. . . I don't know, what about school?"

"It would be safest if you didn't go for the time being," Oliver said. "If you made up a really good excuse, then disappeared for a while." Oliver clapped Jake on the shoulder and led him into the kitchen. "Think about it for a moment. I'll sit with Gaia until she wakes up. It won't be long. You can take the time to get used to all this information."

Jake nodded and went to the kitchen as ordered— another point in his favor. Oliver was interested. Very interested indeed.

He sat on the floor next to Gaia, watching her breathe as she fought off her exhaustion. After about ten minutes, she stirred and opened her eyes. She sat up like a shot, assessing her surroundings with micro-processorlike speed.

"Where's Jake?" she asked.

"He's fine. He's here."

She turned to Oliver. "We got tailed. They saw him," she told him. "He can't—"

"I know. I discussed it with him."

Gaia slumped back down on the couch, letting loose a frustrated sigh. "I should never have gotten him mixed up in this. He'll have to stay here while we're away."

"He could do that. Or. . ."

"What?" Gaia turned to Oliver.

"I got extra travel documents," Oliver said. "An old habit that might work in our favor. He has excellent instincts. Apparently he can hold up his end of a fight. I have a good feeling about him, and we can use an extra agent."

"I don't want him in any deeper than he is already." Gaia insisted. "I mean, I almost got him killed already. Isn't that enough?"

"What if he wants to come?" Oliver asked. "We could leave it up to him."

"Leave what up to me?" Jake appeared in the doorway.

"Forget it. Nothing," Gaia insisted. "Jake, I'm so sorry. I should never have let you come with me. Now you have to—"

"It's all right," Jake said. "I mean, I was the one who insisted on coming."

"What about the other thing? How you can't go home?"

"That sucks," he admitted. "But if you guys are talking about having me come along to. . . wherever it is you're going, I'm in."

"Jake, don't be stupid," Gaia seethed. "This isn't level three of Grand Theft Auto."

"Don't insult me," Jake snapped back. "I've been watching you deal with whatever's been going on for a week now. I'm well aware of how serious it is. But

51

according to Oliver, I've got to sit around, anyway. I'll go nuts here. There's no way I'll stay inside the whole time, and without you here to watch my back, I'll get nabbed for sure. And Gaia—I really want to come with you."

"Even if I'm going to *Siberia*?" she asked.

Siberia?

Quite honestly, if he'd had his pick of locales, Siberia wouldn't have been first—or even ninety-first—on his list, but he'd known better than to expect St. John's or Montego Bay to have any place on Gaia Moore's travel itinerary.

"Look, I know Siberia won't be a picnic. And I think I understand the danger. But it's weird—I feel like this is what I was meant to do. Like this is why I met you—because I'm supposed to do stuff like this. I'll never know if I don't try."

While Gaia turned herself into a knot of deep sighs and fevered hand gestures, Oliver gave meditative consideration to Jake's response.

"You don't seem frightened by this," he said.

Jake looked at him. "I know, it's weird. I'm not."

"We'd be leaving within twelve hours," Oliver said. "You wouldn't be able to see your father again before you left." He shrugged. "That's the bottom line."

"I can do it."

"Jake!" Gaia was exasperated. "You don't know what you're saying. This is dangerous."

"More dangerous than getting shot at, or outrunning a fake police officer and his cronies?" Jake asked. "So far, I've been able to handle it."

"It's worse than all of that. Jake, I was thrown into this world. You don't have to be in it. Are you crazy?"

"I don't think so. Do you think I am, Oliver?"

"Not as far as I can tell."

Gaia gave an infuriated roar. "I've seen a lot of people I care about get destroyed by being close to me," she said. "I've seen them ruined by this life. I don't want you to do this."

"But I'm in it," Jake said. "Look, let me get fully informed. Then I'll make my decision. But it's *my* decision. You can't get pissed at me for being okay with this."

"Watch me," Gaia muttered, and left the room.

Jake turned to Oliver. "Is she right? Am I destroying myself without thinking this through?"

"I've had a lot of experience with a lot of different kinds of operatives," Oliver said. "I've seen men who trained for years fall apart under questioning, and I've seen the most unlikely people turn into heroes. I don't think anyone chooses this life consciously. I think it's something you're born to. And much as Gaia claims to hate it, I think she has grown to be comfortable with danger and chaos. You might be cut from the same cloth."

"Might be?"

"This trip will be sort of a test for you."

"And what if I fail?"

Oliver shrugged. "Then you might want to return to life the way it was. I think you'll be able to, despite Gaia's protestations to the contrary."

Jake thought it over. Between Gaia and Oliver, it was certainly Oliver who had the most experience. If Oliver felt confident in Jake, that was really all the information he needed. Well, that, and one other tiny detail.

"Well then, guys, there's only one other thing I need to know."

"What's that, son?" asked Oliver.

Jake paused dramatically. "What the hell are we going to Siberia for?"

I can't imagine what it feels like to be Gaia. I mean, everybody goes through life thinking they're the only person who feels the way they do. But in Gaia's case, she might be right. If my dad were in captivity in Siberia, I'm not sure I'd be prepared to go save him. I'm not sure I could keep it together, knowing that my father's very survival depended solely on my ability to pull off a great escape.

On the other hand, whether she admits it or not, I'm the perfect person to help Gaia rescue *her* father. Maybe it's being the son of a doctor who spent years in the ER. Or maybe it's all my martial arts training. But in all honesty, I always manage to keep a level head in situations that send other people into a panic.

Don't get me wrong: I'm not so naïve as to think that believing I'm good at something means that I actually am. Just look at *American Idol*. All those people think they're destined for stardom. Most aren't even destined for a gig at the Holiday Inn lounge.

I have no idea what's going to happen to me in Siberia. But I'm not that worried about it. Maybe that means I really am crazy. Or maybe it means I always knew this would happen to me. It's like in *The Matrix*: The blue pill is always the way to go. Maybe I should be frightened of the unknown, but I'm not. I'm psyched. This really is what I want. My life has always been stable. I think I need to shake things up and see if I'm right. If I've got what it takes.

Am I going to feel the same way tomorrow? Am I just being impulsive? Am I making a life-changing move based on overactive hormones? I don't think so.

Jeez, I hope not.

Guess there's only one way to find out.

And while I'm at it, maybe I'll find out why Gaia's father was taken to Siberia in the first place.

Maybe.

But probably not.

This couldn't have happened at a better time. My biggest worry over the past days—a worry that haunted me at every turn—was that we didn't have enough manpower to complete this mission. All I kept wishing for was an extra agent. Someone who'd watch Gaia's back just in case something happened to me. Much as I would love to be alone with her, my instincts told me we needed someone else.

And now this boy shows up, as if my prayers had been heard and answered.

It seems foolhardy. I don't know this boy very well. I've got no reason to trust him, other than those same instincts. But Gaia found him. She brought him here. There must be a reason for that. She is careful and suspicious enough to avoid trusting anyone until he has fully proven himself. Nobody knows that better than I do. And she's impatient enough to avoid anyone foolish or

frivolous. I have a very good
feeling about this young man.

And what if something goes
drastically wrong? What if he
cracks under pressure, makes an
impulsive mistake, turns into a
blubbering fool halfway through
the mission?

This is where my instincts disappear. My Loki instinct would be
to neutralize him. And my Oliver
instinct? I don't know how I'd
handle the situation now.

I'll just have to hope that's
not a problem I'll have to face.
For his sake. And for Gaia's.

And let's face it: for mine, too.

THE NEXT MORNING, GAIA AND JAKE

A Gaia— Sized Gap

left Oliver's building separately, walking in different directions and meeting up only after their train had taken them into Manhattan. They'd woken in silence, sipping coffee in the kitchen with Oliver without speaking. Now Jake noticed that Gaia really didn't want to talk. The ease, the friendship that had only just developed between them, seemed gone already.

"You're mad at me," he said.

"No, I'm worried," Gaia answered.

"It's okay. I understand the risks. I'm not getting dragged into this against my will."

"I just hope you're doing it for the right reasons."

Jake was quiet for a moment. "I've never had a chance like this. To go somewhere crazy and do something so out of the ordinary. I'm really into it."

Gaia shook her head. "And you think you can deal with your dad?" she asked.

"Yeah, I'll come up with a good cover story," Jake reassured her.

"And what about last night? Don't you think he's wondering why you never came home?"

"Nah, he was on call. That's the advantage of having an ER doctor for a dad," Jake explained.

They were within a block of his house. Together with Oliver, they had mapped out the area as best they could from Jake's memory, noting adjacent buildings and points of access. A few blueprints, downloaded from a confidential site Oliver had gained access to, didn't hurt either. They found the building around the corner that they needed, and Gaia stepped back and took a look up.

"Hm. Pretty good security," she said.

"Too good?"

"Nah. I'd climb the outside if it weren't broad daylight. We're going in through the basement."

"But the bars. . ."

"Watch."

Gaia sprayed each end of one of the bars with a canister she took out of her pocket. Then she straightened up and hooked her thumbs into the belt loops of her jeans, waiting.

"That's your big trick?" Jake asked. "You're deodorizing the bars?"

"Just wait."

After a minute she brought her foot down on the bar and it snapped easily, leaving a `Gaia-sized gap` through which she could reach in and smash the basement window. She slipped through and vanished into the room below.

"Hey," Jake said in a stage whisper. "Hey! I can't fit in there!"

The spray-canister flew out the hole and landed on the sidewalk with a clatter. He picked it up and sprayed two more of the bars.

"Where did you get this stuff, anyway?" he asked, kneeling on the concrete while he waited for it to take effect and weaken the metal.

"Gift from my Uncle Oliver," her voice floated up through the gloom. "Guess it was left over from his secret agent days."

"That's a catalog I'd like to have a look at." He stood up and kicked the other two bars out of his way and shimmied into the basement.

He held onto the bars for a moment, then dropped to the ground, expecting to land on a dusty floor. He hit linoleum instead.

"What the—"

Gaia laughed and snapped the light on. "I guess someone uses this as an office or a classroom or something," she said. "'Always speak in your inside voice,'" Gaia said, mocking the poster that hung in front of the room.

"Very helpful. Now how do we get from here to my apartment?"

"The two buildings share an air shaft. We need to get in there and climb up."

Across the hall, in the interior of the building, another room had a painted-over window. "I'll bet that's where we want to be," Gaia said. She knocked against it a

61

few times with her fist. When it wouldn't budge, she stood on a chair and scraped away the layers of paint. Then she wiggled the overpainted hasps until they gave. The window popped open with a creak.

She slid out the window easily and found herself in a gloomy area about the size of a studio apartment, cluttered with decades' worth of garbage. She heard something scuttling around her feet and willed herself not to look down. Jake joined her. They could see blue sky far above, but here, at the bottom of four flights of brick, the sun never shone.

"You had to live on the top floor?" Gaia asked.

"If I'd known, I would have moved into that basement," he said. "Would have made this a lot easier, I know. And it was pretty nice."

"Do you know how to rock-climb?"

"I think you know the answer to that. But our shoes are all wrong."

"I know—I think we have to do this barefoot."

"Okay, now that's gross."

"See? I knew you couldn't handle it."

Jake squinted at Gaia and pulled off his sneakers and socks. Then, without another word, he found a handhold between two loose bricks and began his journey upward.

"I wish we had some rappelling line," Gaia muttered, then tied her own sneakers around her neck and followed him up.

It took an amazing amount of concentration. Gaia was an expert climber, but finding impressions on a rock wall was a lot easier than dealing with the repetitive bricks and their limited shapes and sizes. It was even slower going for Jake.

"I don't think anyone would have spotted me going into the building," he said, as he wrestled his way toward the window of his apartment.

"Shows what you know," Gaia said. She was already up there and was giving the window frame a few exploratory thumps. "These aren't even locked," she scolded.

"Yeah, well, it's four flights up, over an air shaft," he pointed out. "How paranoid am I supposed to be?"

"Once again, shows what you know." Gaia's voice floated out through the open window; she had opened the window noiselessly and slipped inside in the space of a few seconds. Jake shook his head. Amazing.

A rope ladder—Jake recognized it as his family's never-used fire-escape plan—came tumbling down the wall, almost knocking Jake off balance.

"Hey!" he yelled. "What am I supposed to do with this?"

"I thought it would be good if you could get up here before the end of the year," Gaia suggested. "Just use it—you don't have to prove anything to me."

"I'm not trying to prove anything to you," he said. "I don't know how to use the rope."

Gaia's head appeared two stories above him, black against the bright sky and framed in hanks of hair. "Jake, just grab it with one hand. You won't fall." Her voice was so matter-of-fact, Jake felt she was acting as if she'd ordered the laws of gravity to suspend themselves. Any minute now, she'd lose her patience. Jake's slow climb obviously wasn't cutting the mustard. He was going to have to take the risk.

From now on, he was always going to have to take the risk—at least, for the next few days, if he wanted to keep up.

He let go with his left hand and felt his center of gravity shift. He was going to fall for sure. The lurch in his stomach told him so.

He grabbed a rung of the ladder.

He got it.

And he hung on for dear life.

"Okay, Montone." He was going to have to be his own cheering section. He tried to do it coolly, under his breath, but he heard it come out in a squeak.

"Jake!" Gaia hissed from above. There was no more time to be nervous. Jake clutched the ladder and swung his body completely onto it, letting go of the safety of his tiny foot- and handholds and making a huge leap of faith. He scrambled up the ladder as quickly as he could.

His apartment was silent. He hadn't lived here that long with his dad, but it was still home, still filled with stuff that had followed him wherever he'd lived. The rich wool Oriental rug that had been a wedding gift to his parents, the dark wood furniture and the photos of his family. But even in these familiar surroundings, Jake felt like he was trespassing. Why was that?

Well, because he was. He wasn't supposed to be here. He'd come to say good-bye.

"Come on," Gaia said quietly, like she could tell he was having a moment of strangeness. "Get whatever you need, and let's go."

Jake gathered some warm clothes, the bare minimum he'd need, and his toothbrush. His dad. It was time to make the call.

He sat down at the dining-room table and picked up the phone. His dad had given him a lot of freedom, so that he wouldn't have to lie. Now he was going to. He dialed the number at his dad's office and had the receptionist put him through.

"Dad, I got a call," he said. "Remember that tae kwan do competition in Montreal I went to last year? They had a last-minute emergency and they need me to be a judge."

Jake felt weird lying to his father in front of Gaia. He was revealing a side of himself that wasn't necessarily the most attractive.

"How'd that go?" Gaia asked when he hung up the phone.

Jake looked down for a long moment. He felt

exposed. "Fine," he finally said. "Let's get out of here. Back out the window, barefoot, right?"

"Right."

Back out the window, barefoot. That sounded like a recipe for disaster if there ever was one.

It also sounded like Gaia's life in a nutshell.

ED FARGO SPOTTED AN ENEMY AGENT

stepping out from behind a column on the subway platform. He raised his gun and shot as fast as he could—but the bullets wouldn't come out fast enough.

Ping-Pong

"Where's my Glock?" he shrieked. "Oh my God, I can't get to my Glock! What's going on?"

Somehow he fumbled. His fingers wouldn't go where he wanted them to, and he watched helplessly as the enemy agent fired again and again and again. His vision went red, and then he was dead.

"Dude," Kai said. "You are the worst Xbox player ever."

"Well, excuse me," he shot back. "I spent my childhood skateboarding, not getting fat on Nintendo."

Kai nodded in that way she had, where she kind of ducked her head twice and gave a slow blink. Ed snapped off the video game and Kai's living room flickered into darkness. The only light came from the neon restaurant sign outside the window. It buzzed a little. Somehow that made the silence a little more oppressive.

"So," he said. "You play that game a lot?"

"I guess, yeah."

"It's pretty good."

"Yeah, I like it."

"They uh. . . they got a lot of the New York details right. There's nothing weird, like all of a sudden the Brooklyn Bridge goes to Jersey."

"Yeah, right." Kai gave a laugh. But she didn't add to the thought. Ed didn't know what he wanted her to say. But *something* would have been nice.

"So."

"Yeah?"

"What do you want to do?"

Kai shrugged. "I don't know. What do you want to do?"

The dreaded ping-pong question of two bored people. Ed cringed. But he couldn't think of anything. They had seen every movie there was to see. They had done everything adventurous there was to do. There was no activity available to them besides hanging out, and that wasn't going too well.

"We could make out," Kai suggested.

Ed looked at her. She was adorable. Her shiny, sleek

black hair fell to her shoulders, with two pigtails at her temples held up with Hello Kitty clips. He could see that under her white baby tee and army pants she had a seriously smokin' body. Of course, as a red-blooded American male, he was completely willing to spend his hanging-out time tongue-wrestling with a cute skateboard girl.

"Okay," he said, and smooched her.

But there was something unelectric about the whole thing. Sure, her lips were soft. Yeah, his body responded to hers as they lay together on the plaid couch. And he liked Kai. This was fun and all, but something was missing from the whole equation.

Kai was great to do stuff with, but the minute there was a lull, Ed had to admit it: There just wasn't much of a spark.

Oh, no.

Heather. Gaia. Tatiana. What did they all have in common? They all drove him crazy with their various insane behaviors. Bitchy, moody, or just plain schizophrenic, each one of them had a serious personality disorder that gave him a constant case of acid reflux.

And now he was addicted to them. He knew it. He was addicted to the frustration. Ed Fargo had completely, utterly lost the ability to be with a regular girl.

He shifted positions so that he was on top of Kai. She moved along with him willingly and opened her eyes long enough to smile at him between kisses. She ran her hands up under his shirt and he tried to stay in the moment.

Stop thinking about them, he ordered himself. *You're making out with a cute girl. Who cares about them? Who cares about Gaia, especially? You are making out, Fargo. Come on!*

"Come on," Kai said, sitting up. "We can go in my room. My parents won't be home for hours."

Ed followed her into her room, decorated with standard-issue posters of Green Day and System of a Down.

"What's up?" Kai asked him. "You nervous?"

"No, it's cool," he said.

"Cool." She stripped off her top and sat on her bed. "Come on, then."

He followed her over to the bed, smiling reassuringly, but he felt like a jerk. This was the most uninspired he'd ever been. What they were doing felt mechanical, cold. All it did was remind him how great it had been with Gaia. He kissed Kai one last time, closing his eyes and trying to enjoy it, but it was no use. He sat up.

"Oh, man," Kai said. "Now what?"

"I just remembered, my mom needs me at home," he said. "I'm supposed to. . . do something."

"Ed, what's wrong?" Kai sat up. "Is something bothering you? Is it me?"

"No! No, it's most definitely not you. It's one

hundred percent me," Ed insisted. He shook his head. "You're perfect. You're awesome, you're a great girl. I just forgot about this thing. My mom really needs me at home."

Kai peered up at him as though she wasn't sure whether she should believe him. She seemed a little hurt. But she didn't hit him with a stormy accusation, which was a relief. It was also a little strange.

"Well, okay," she said, pulling her shirt back on. "I guess I'll see you tomorrow, right?"

"Right!" he said. "Tomorrow. Yes." Ed got up and grabbed his skateboard. "I'm really sorry I've got to go like this. That was really, you know. . ."

"Yeah! Totally!" Kai nodded. "Come on, I'll walk you out."

Ed kissed Kai and left her apartment. The fact that she hadn't started a big argument about his having to leave so unexpectedly—it sort of threw him. He wondered if she was supposed to get more upset. Or maybe she was just normal, and he was too screwed up to know the difference? That was what he was really worried about. What if his sense of normal had been warped by his history of nutty girlfriends?

He looked up and saw the lights of a plane shooting slowly across the sky. Gaia leapt into his consciousness again, for about the fortieth time that night. Maybe because that plane was a mile away, like she always was. Maybe it was the blinking of its lights, switching on and off like her feelings for him. Or maybe she'd been on his mind already, and anything he looked at was going to make him think of her.

Oh, man. When was he going to get Gaia Moore out of his system?

So Gaia's in my system, like a virus. She moves around inside me, popping up when I least expect her. And she's not showing any signs of leaving on her own.

I wonder how you get rid of something like this? I wonder how I'm supposed to track down all the little Gaia-modules among my platelets and obliterate them? Maybe I should just envision the process as a video game. Every time she pops up, I'll blast her out of me. It'll be like Whack-a-Mole.

No, that's too New Agey. I think I need some medical intervention. I need a doctor to find some Gaia antibodies. Some kind of serum that'll flush her out of my system.

Or maybe I should just go sit in a hot sauna and sweat her out of me. Maybe a high fever would burn her out. Maybe, with enough coffee, I could pee her out.

I don't know, though. If it were that easy, I guess hotels and spas would offer Love-Cleansing Weekends, where they'd give you a high colonic and you'd leave with no lingering love whatsoever. If it were that easy, people wouldn't write songs and poems and novels about their lost loves. If it were that easy. . . I'd be making out with Kai right now.

I think I'll have the Gaia virus for a long time. I'm just going to have to learn to live with it and all the accompanying symptoms: memories popping into my head at inopportune moments, lack of interest in other girls, the burning curiosity about what she's doing and who she's doing it with. I have to treat Gaia like a long-lasting but manageable disease. Like a heart murmur. Like arthritis. Like diabetes.

That's it. I've got Gaiabetes. Hah.

The thing is, there's only one person who would think that was funny. Only one person on the planet I could share that joke with. And you know who that is.

Gaia.

Oh, man. Someone get me some insulin.

It was difficult for Gaia to reconcile this **not** kind man with **in** her image **kansas** of the **anymore** serial killer formerly known as Loki.

GAIA TURNED AROUND IN HER AIR-

eminiscence

plane seat and peered over the top at Jake. He had pushed his seat all the way back and was snoring with his mouth open. She sat back down and turned to Oliver.

"If sleeping were an Olympic sport, I think he'd be heading for the gold right about now," she said.

"It's very impressive. I wish I could sleep like that. Years of being an agent really trained it out of me," Oliver told her. "That coma was the first uninterrupted sleep I've had since I was in my twenties."

"So it was good for something."

"It was good for a lot of things." Oliver gave her a look. "It brought me back to you."

"I like how they show the movies on the backs of the seats now," Gaia said. She wasn't ignoring Oliver's overture purposely. She just didn't know how to respond to people when they said sweet things to her.

"Yes, but with all that new technology, they couldn't come up with better entertainment?"

Gaia laughed. "You didn't like the feature presentation?"

Oliver shook his head. "Those kids might be easy on the eyes, but they both looked embarrassed in that last scene. Like they didn't want to be there any more than I wanted to be watching them."

"The romantic comedy," Gaia said. "Boy meets girl,

boy loses girl, girl comes to her senses. . . boy and girl get paycheck."

They both laughed. It wasn't that funny, but the flight was long, and they still felt a little uneasy with each other.

"We need to come up with our cover story," Oliver said.

Gaia was relieved to have something businesslike to talk about. "Yeah, I guess we can't announce to customs that we're there to rescue my secret agent father from kidnappers."

"Especially since we don't know how deep this goes. Anyone we meet could be in on this. We don't know who has him, exactly, and the government of Siberia could be involved."

Gaia hadn't thought of that. "Do they know we're coming?"

"I don't think so, but we have to be prepared for anything. When we go through customs, we should say we're all one family. The passports have the same last name, so we should be all right."

"Sounds like a great plan. I'll try to be very sisterly toward Jake."

"It shouldn't be hard. You two seem like good friends."

"I guess we are. And it shouldn't be too difficult for you to play my dad. You're his twin—it's not exactly a stretch."

Oliver became quiet. His face blurred into an expression Gaia couldn't quite read. "What's wrong?"

"Oh, nothing."

"Something. What is it?"

"It's just—" Oliver shook his head. "When you said that, I had such a clear memory of you as a baby. At about four months old. You know, that's when babies start having real personalities."

"I wouldn't know." Gaia grimaced. "Babies."

"Oh, but you were a wonderful baby," Oliver told her. "You always had this wise expression. This wide-open smile. You woke up with that smile, like you were excited to see what the world had in store for you. My adoration for you was only obscured by my envy for my brother."

This reminiscence made Gaia's skin crawl. By the time Gaia was born, Oliver had been forbidden from visiting her parents' home. The only way he'd have had any idea what she was like as a baby would be if he had seen her behind her parents' back. This minor detail had obviously slipped Oliver's mind just then. But it reminded Gaia that the man she was dealing with was both twisted and tragic.

"That was my biggest mistake," Oliver continued. "Instead of tormenting myself with envy, I should have made my own life. Though I wouldn't have been able to have a child. And even if I could have. . ." He shot an embarrassed smile at Gaia. "Well, I just don't see how she could have been more wonderful than you."

It was difficult for Gaia to reconcile this kind man with her image of the serial killer formerly known as Loki. On the other hand, he clearly loved with the same frightening intensity that he'd hated with. And the last thing Gaia needed right now was more intensity.

"Oliver, come on. Don't you think we should catch up on our sleep?" Gaia asked gently, hoping that her suggestion wouldn't be taken as an insult. The irony of the scenario could have blown her mind if Gaia had let it. Here she was, protecting the feelings of the very man who'd taken her mother's life in cold blood. But now wasn't exactly the time to contemplate life's little curiosities.

The plane hummed though a bank of clouds, and Gaia put her headphones on and closed her eyes. She looked over at Jake, who was passed out and drooling. At the moment she could think of nothing more appealing than joining him. Something told her there wouldn't be a lot of time for sleep once they got there.

THE RUSSIAN AIRPORT WAS AS different from JFK as an airport could be. About the only thing they had in common were the A Recor airplanes. The New York airport had a mall's worth of food shops and magazine stands. This place was clean, but it was distinctly more low-rent than the gleaming American version. It was clear to Gaia that she was not in Kansas anymore.

They hadn't checked any luggage, so she, Oliver, and Jake hitched their carry-ons onto their shoulders and began strolling toward the exit.

"*Tsst, tsst.* You vont cab, nice lady?" A slimy-looking guy approached them, wearing a shoopy-sounding vinyl tracksuit and sporting a moustache that would have made a porn star proud.

"No, thanks." Gaia shook her head, and Oliver and Jake moved in more closely to her. She looked around for security guards, but there didn't seem to be any. As they stepped out through the sliding glass doors, Gaia got the very distinct feeling that something wasn't right.

"You vont cab, yes?" The guy sidled up to them again, and this time he had a friend. A beefy friend.

"No," Oliver said firmly. Jake looked at him, waiting for a sign that they should fight. But Gaia knew the sign wouldn't come. Not now. They were trying to avoid detection. And getting in a fracas—that would be a dead giveaway. Three tourists with fighting skills like theirs? Not likely.

"This way," Oliver said, and led them back toward the airport door. Their way was blocked by two more locals. They eyeballed Oliver, Jake, and Gaia as though they were adding up how much everything they were carrying would net them in resale.

"Dangerous to leave airport without a cab," the first guy said. "Not safe. I know these men; I can help you get away from them."

"Yes, all right," Oliver said. "Let's get into the cab. Can you put this in the trunk?" He acted as if he were handing the guy his tote bag, then swung it into his face and turned to run.

"Come on!" he shouted, but Gaia and Jake were already heading along the sidewalk to the well-populated area on the other side of the airport.

Gaia heard their shouts as her feet thudded along the pavement. She'd been here five minutes and was already in trouble. This had to be a record.

"Who are those guys?" she shouted to Oliver.

"Nobody," he shouted back, as they rounded a corner and saw a clot of black cars and security guards. Lord only knew what godforsaken corner of the airport they'd wandered into. Bad rescue party. Bad!

Oliver slowed them down and looked behind him. Their four local assailants were standing in a forlorn-looking huddle; the big beefy guy lit a cigarette in defeat. Then they turned and headed back to the side exit of the airport.

"Those are some brazen muggers," Jake said. "Are you sure they're not after us specifically?"

Oliver shook his head. "There's no way. Men like

that seem to pop up wherever there are tourists, over here. They're leftovers from the old Soviet Union."

"It's good we didn't fight them, then," Gaia said. "Too bad, though. It would have been easy."

Oliver patted her on the shoulder. "That's my girl," he said, shaking his head.

Oliver got in the front seat of the cab and murmured to the driver in expert-sounding Russian. Despite the seriousness of their mission, Gaia felt something. . . nice. Comfortable. She knew she was on her way to her dad, and she was making the trip with people who seemed to know her. To understand her. Well enough to tease her, in fact. In spite of her annoyance, she looked out the window and smiled.

"Cheerleading team," she muttered out loud. "You guys can go to hell."

I know I'm on a serious mission. I know that at any moment we could be attacked and I could be in the fight of my life. Worse, I know that this journey to find my father could end in horrible disappointment.

So why do I feel so. . . almost normal?

Maybe it's the anticipation, the closeness of the possibility that I'm going to see my dad. Or maybe. . . just maybe. . . being with Oliver and Jake actually feels comfortable to me. Maybe I'm actually learning to trust people.

Two of them, anyway.

It's the strangest thing. Oliver I have no reason to trust, except that he's spent the past few days trying desperately to prove himself to me. I mean, every once in a while I get a bit of a freaky feeling from him, but let's face it: Evil or kind, he's kind of a freak. And Jake I've only known for a few weeks. Yet

every time I need to rely on
either of them, they seem to come
through for me. Maybe that's par
for the course on planet Earth.
But on planet Gaia, it's unheard
of. In fact, it's downright
against the laws of nature.

I actually have to will myself
to pull back, feel less, trust
less, be more suspicious. That's
never happened before. It's like
my polar ice caps are melting.
Global warming, you might say.

So the question remains: Is
this a new springtime for me? Or
is it an ecological disaster of
world-ending proportions? I won't
know till this is over.

I wish I could just relax and
enjoy it in the meantime.

But if that were possible, it
wouldn't be planet Gaia.

GAIA, JAKE, AND OLIVER SETTLED

into their four-seat compartment on the train. The station itself was gorgeous—pink marble, arched ceilings, and amazing Russian architecture. Gaia had to admit it: The place was almost as grand as Grand Central. But the trains themselves—at least the one that was destined to travel southeast, to Siberia—were decidedly less grand. On this one, she, Oliver, and Jake had passed down a narrow corridor, squeezed between aged wooden walls, and now found themselves sitting on red vinyl seats with their knees touching. A Formica table folded out from the wall, and a well-used pack of cards sat in a magazine holder, along with a copy of *Mademoiselle* from 1998.

"This is cozy," Gaia said.

"It smells like old socks," Jake pointed out.

"I think that's actually the food."

"If you think this is rough, you'd have made horrible agents," Oliver told them. "I've had to eat creatures you'd both call an exterminator to get rid of."

"Nice," Gaia said.

"What's the grossest thing you ever ate?"

Oliver thought for a moment. "Termites. I really didn't like the termites. I tried to swallow them whole and they moved around in my throat. But crunching them was worse. It was a lose-lose situation."

"Termites." Gaia shrugged. "I'd rather eat something small than have to bite into a big water bug."

"I ate those in the Philippines. They're not so bad if you batter-fry them."

"Mmm, this conversation is making me hungry," Oliver said. "Let me see if there's a cafeteria car on this train. If I can't find anything, we'll have to dip into our rations, but I'd rather save those for an emergency."

"Don't go too far," Gaia said. "I wouldn't even know how to start looking for you." The face she turned up to him was struggling to remain impassive, but both Jake and Oliver could see she wasn't sure of herself, not at all. Fearlessness was one thing—emotionlessness was another. Maybe it was the huge scope of this mission, or maybe it was the stress of finally getting near her father—she was showing signs of wear and tear. It made them both feel very, very protective.

"Don't worry," Oliver promised. "I won't even touch the food if it looks dangerous."

Gaia pulled her feet up under her in her seat and turned back to Jake. "So I think we have some time to kill," she said.

"About twelve hours or so."

"What are we going to do?"

"I'd say we could play poker, but this deck only has fifty cards."

"Well, that's an interesting metaphor," Gaia muttered, taking the deck and shuffling through it to count the cards herself. "Sometimes I don't think anybody's playing with a full deck."

"Funny," Jake said.

"Then why aren't you laughing?"

"Because it's not, really."

He went silent and sat back, looking out the window. Gaia appreciated that: the quiet, without the awkward silence. The chugging of the train along the tracks, in a mesmerizing rhythm, was the only conversation. Gaia counted the cards again, and again. Then she started sorting them into suits, in order. Then a distant memory made a ghost of a smile flit across her face.

"What?" Jake asked.

"Oh, I don't know."

"Come on. I'm bored."

Gaia rolled her eyes. "When I was a kid, I had a deck of cards that was, like, ancient. And a couple were missing. But I wanted to learn to play cards, so. . . someone made the extra ones out of those index cards. You know, the ones people use to take notes on?"

"The ones David Letterman throws at the audience," Jake added.

"I guess. Anyway, so there were, like, forty-nine cards, and then these three bright white ones with the suits and numbers written on them, so whenever you tried to play anything, it was so obvious that the other person had a nine of clubs or whatever. It just didn't work." Gaia gave a quiet laugh. "I guess it's not really funny, it's just—it was funny that we thought it would work in the first place."

"It *is* kind of funny," Jake said. "Who did that, your dad?"

"Oh, no. It was. . . someone else." Gaia studied her cards.

"I mean, duh."

"What?"

"Obviously it was your mom."

Gaia's forehead wrinkled slightly, as if a headache were whooshing through it, then smoothed as if nothing had happened.

"Yeah. My dad was too organized and anal to come up with a goofy plan like that."

"You've never talked about her. Not to me, anyway."

Gaia shrugged.

"I'll tell you about mine."

"You don't have to."

"Okay."

Jake went silent again. Gaia reorganized the cards yet again, this time putting the two black suits together before moving on to the red. She marveled at how interesting a pack of cards could become when you needed a distraction. Something to keep you from blurting out your feelings in some kind of ill-advised self-revelatory soul-vomit. She forced herself to put the cards down and leaned back in her seat, putting her sneakers up on Jake's side of the compartment.

Cha-chug. Cha-chug. Cha-chug.

"I don't remember her as well as I'm supposed to," she mumbled. "I mean, I knew her until I was twelve. It's not like she—it's not like I lost her when I was a baby." It was a good lie. It kept Gaia from having to reopen the wounds, and it was believable enough. Jake couldn't possibly know about Gaia's sterling memory.

"The memories fade a little," Jake agreed, without pressing further. "It's disappointing."

Cha-chug. Cha-chug. Cha-chug.

"Did you, uh. . . I mean, do you ever think about stuff you said? To her? Your mom?" asked Gaia.

"You mean bad stuff? Like when I acted like a baby?" Jake asked.

"Well, you *were* a baby. But yeah."

"Um, I guess I do. But my dad sent me to a therapist for a while, right after it happened. And the therapist kept telling me that I was just acting like a normal kid, and that my mom knew I didn't really think she was a giant mean poo-head."

Gaia gave a snorting laugh. "Well, you got your money's worth out of that therapist."

"I know." Jake laughed, too. "But I gave myself a really hard time, anyway. I think I replayed every bratty moment I ever had with her, after she was gone. I was sure that I had made her life absolute hell."

"Huh."

The cards became fascinating again. This time, Gaia started poking them into the space between the glass window and the wall so that they stood plastered against the scenery outside. Then she studied the king, queen, and jack of diamonds as they stood there, gazing calmly back at her like a little nuclear family.

"Yeah," she said.

"What?"

"I can see how you'd do that."

Cha-chug. Cha-chug. Cha-chug.

"Did you do that?" Jake hazarded.

Gaia looked up at him, then snatched the cards out of the window and put them back into the deck.

"Forget I asked," he said.

"Sorry." Gaia gave an apologetic shrug. "It's not something I ever talk about. But the last conversation we had was a fight."

"You and your mom?"

"Yeah. I mean, I was twelve. Have you ever met a twelve-year-old? They're horrible."

"I'm sure you weren't—"

"Oh, please."

Jake laughed. "Well, I guess judging from the Gaia I know now, you might have been a tiny bit difficult."

"I was just annoyed all the time. Pissed off around

the clock. My body was doing all these wacky things, and my training was going horribly."

"I think that's normal."

"Yeah, maybe."

Gaia was silent as she remembered the rest of it. The whole idea of becoming a woman had freaked her out. She'd thought her boobs looked like fat blobs, and her center of gravity had been totally off. And her hips—she couldn't shop in the boy's department anymore. Her mom had seemed so comfortable in her skin, so beautiful and perfect; Gaia had seen herself as a ridiculous imitation. But she hadn't been able to find the words to explain how she felt, so she'd just acted like a bratty bitch.

The morning her mother died, Gaia had thrown a fit over something. God, she couldn't remember what. Breakfast, maybe? She'd wanted coffee and her mom had insisted on something more substantial. That's what moms do. And Gaia had acted like she was being asked to eat worms. She'd flown into a rage and left the house to go for a run. Loki had pulled the trigger just as Gaia had stepped back into the house. Her mom was dead before Gaia ever had a chance to apologize to her.

Gaia had never told anyone about that fight with her mother. In fact, even when she thought back to that day, she rarely touched on that episode. She felt too ashamed. What had she been so angry about? Why hadn't she—?

"You know, if you buy a pack of cards in Italy,

there's no queen," Jake said, taking the pile of cards from the seat next to Gaia and handing it to her. She took it gratefully and started shuffling them back into random order.

"No kidding," she said.

"Yeah, these are American cards. Or British."

"Why would you know that?"

Jake shrugged. "I have no idea. It's just a random fact stuck in my head."

Gaia envied Jake's state of mind. He seemed so relaxed and carefree. Why did she have to be so somber? Why was she forever wreathed in deep thought and regret? It wasn't as if Jake hadn't had tragedy in his life. And yet here he was, fully capable of levity. Why *was* she thinking of this now? Because she was missing her dad? Because she was bored and had too much time on her hands? Or was it because Jake made her feel comfortable enough for old feelings to bubble to the surface?

Ugh. If that were the case, Gaia was in big trouble. Now was *not* the time to start getting comfortable with Jake. She was glad when the feeling started to dissipate and she could think about something else.

"I hope you don't regret coming along," Gaia said to Jake.

"I don't," he said. "This is way more exciting than going to school. Besides, how could I miss all of this?" He waved his hand, taking in the dingy compartment, the musty smell, and the grimy window.

"I didn't mean for you to get sucked into my screwed-up world."

"I'm not sucked in. I'm fine."

"Well, I'm not." Gaia returned to studying the scene outside her windows, trees whipping by too quickly to discern one from the next, while mountains sat serenely in the distance. "After this, I want to chill out. For a long time."

"What's a long time?" Jake asked, arching an eyebrow. "You wouldn't last a weekend without a crisis to distract you."

"Try me. Try me and see how happy I'd be."

They rode in silence again. Friendship settled over them like a blanket, making the silence relaxing and not awkward. When Oliver slipped back into the compartment, they both just looked up at him, unsurprised.

"I got some sandwiches," he said apologetically. "I'm not sure what's in them, exactly."

Gaia bit into one and chewed thoughtfully. "I'm not going to think about it too hard," she said.

"Good move."

"Can't I just wait for the rations?" Jake said.

"No. Here, eat. Jake, we're going to be arriving at Obestoblak in about two hours," Oliver said. "Gaia and I will travel from there to the prison on snowmobiles."

"Oh, awesome," Gaia cheered.

"I want you to stay in town and wait for us," Oliver went on. "There's no reason for you to come along. You haven't been trained for this kind of mission, and if you want to stay behind and just keep things coordinated there, it would be a great help."

"That's a load of bull," Jake said, realizing a little too late that he needed to show Oliver the proper respect. "And I mean that with all due respect, sir. You don't need to make up phony excuses about needing things coordinated. Just level with me."

"Jake!" Gaia shot him an infuriated glare.

"I'm serious. Oliver, if you think I'm going to be a liability, that's one thing. I don't want to drag you down. But I think I can do this, and there's no way I'm going to sit around cooling my jets in a hotel while you guys go up to the prison. I want to come along."

"I don't know if you understand what this entails."

"I understand enough. I want to come along." He held Oliver's gaze steadily.

Finally the older man shrugged and sat down. "Fine. Then we'll spend the next few hours going over the plan. But you'd better not crack under pressure."

"You worry about yourself," Jake said, with that swaggering self-assurance that was beginning to grow on Gaia. Jake was cocky, but at least there was something there to back it up. Which made all the difference in the world.

"I've spoken to some people I used to know in the black market," Oliver told them. "They've put some snowmobiles aside for me, in a shack near the inn where I'm going to take some rooms. . . ."

Gaia listened to the plan as it unfolded. The relaxing motion of the train stopped having its soothing effect. The sound of the wheels slowly turned from a rhythmic lullaby to an energizing drumbeat. They were getting closer to where she needed to be. The battle was about to begin, and like an animal with its hackles up, a domesticated dog whose instincts kick in with a `primal urgency`, she felt her energy start to gather and focus for the task ahead.

She was ready.

I know I'm sitting still, because
my legs aren't moving. My arms are
at my sides and my butt is on a
seat. But I'm also hurtling forward at a hundred and twenty miles
an hour on this train.

My dad told me once that the
worst part about his work was the
waiting. The exciting stuff, he
said, comes in bursts. The rest
of the time you're sitting around
praying for your investigation to
get to the next level or for your
informant to crack and give you
something juicy. If you don't
have patience, you'll never get
anywhere, he told me.

Is that why I'm opening up like
this? Are my feelings rising to
the surface because time is
stretching out before me? Do cops
on stakeouts have major memories
and revelations dogging them in
the wee hours of the morning?

I don't know. But it's kind of
nice to actually feel my feelings, even just a little. It's
cool that Jake doesn't ask for

more. If he did, I'd probably
just clam up.

It's weird, the way my feelings
are just kind of unfolding of
their own accord. Like a complicated reverse origami.

The question is, can I fold
them back up when the action
hits? We're getting closer and
closer to my father, and when the
time comes, I want to be totally
focused. I'm finally going to get
him back, and I don't want to
screw things up with stray emotions that I don't know what to
do with.

How fast is this train going? I
wish it would go faster. Less
time on my hands and more action—
that's the cure.

Only, these feelings. . . they
actually feel kind of good.
Everything in moderation, I
guess.

Together
they used
their
Oliver-
issued
night- **firearms**
vision
goggles to
find their
way through
the snow.

THE INN WAS A RAMSHACKLE STONE

Haphazard Angles

building that sat dejectedly on the outskirts of what Gaia supposed had once passed for a town. Behind it, a weird annex made of prefabricated corrugated sheet metal walls stuck out from one side, making it look as though an alien ship had landed in the wrong place and then abandoned the wreckage in search of a prettier landing spot.

"Definitely not staying here," Jake muttered.

"Look at the mountains, though," Gaia pointed out. In the distance, a range of rocky peaks rose up into clouds so thick, they looked like smoke; they seemed to go on forever. "How close are we?"

"Farther than you think," Oliver said. "But close enough to get there if we can get our hands on the snowmobiles. Come on, let's go see if we can make contact."

They went inside. It seemed like the owners of the inn were trying to imitate an American bar they had seen on a postcard. A Budweiser sign was mounted behind the bar, but it didn't light up—it just sat there, dust covered, like an ancient artifact. The room was dim and smelled like stale smoke and old beer. Metal folding chairs sat at haphazard angles; the bar itself had wooden paneling and a plastic top. It was the most depressing place Gaia had ever seen.

Oliver began speaking in a low voice to the man behind the bar, who eyed him suspiciously. He kept shaking his head. Gaia tried to listen in, but they weren't speaking Russian; it was some kind of dialect. Finally she saw some money exchange hands, and Oliver led them back out into the light of the outside world.

"We have to meet a guy here later," he said.

"Are you sure?" Gaia asked.

"I'm sure that's what this guy told me. Am I sure that's what we're going to do? No," he said. He led them around to the prefabricated annex.

"This is their idea of expanding the property," he explained. "Nobody stays here but traveling tradesmen, so there's no need to impress the tourists. These are guest rooms. This whole area's been poor for a thousand years. There's nothing you can't get for a few dollars, but they're also used to getting as much as they can for the money. They'd rather kill us and take all our money than trade with us and just get some of it."

As if on cue, the man from the bar stepped out into the cold yard and stood eyeing them. Then he motioned for Oliver to join him inside again. Gaia made a move to follow, but Oliver put a hand on her arm.

"Stay here," he said. "Check around back and see if you can find the snowmobiles. I'm pretty sure they're going to be in that garage over there."

A cracked concrete structure stood under a huddle of trees. Gaia nodded and waited until her uncle had gone back inside the building to walk over and peer inside. Sure enough, two snowmobiles sat under tarps in the gloom.

"How old are those things?" Jake whispered.

"I don't know, did Edsel make a snowmobile?" Gaia answered. "At least they won't have a lot of fancy bells and whistles to figure out. Come on."

She stepped into the gloom and found a can of gasoline, which she used to fill up the two tanks. She was getting impatient. Oliver needed to come out here, now. If they couldn't buy or bargain for these vehicles, they should just take them.

Jake stood outside, keeping watch.

"Gaia," he said in a low voice.

"Yeah?"

"Can you get those started?"

"Yeah, I think so. Why?"

A shot rang out, and Gaia stopped asking questions. She revved up her engine, and Jake jumped on the other snowmobile; they shoved them forward, busting through the flimsy and ancient garage door, and shot out into the diamond-white snowy field.

Oliver was running toward them, his backpack flapping behind him like a cape; Gaia pulled up next to him, not even stopping as he hopped on behind her, and maneuvered away from the inn, where the bar guy and two friends were yelling and shaking firearms at them.

"Making friends?" she shouted, as she followed Oliver's pointing finger up a pathway in the woods.

"I paid them, but it wasn't quite enough," he shouted back. "They wanted more. That's what we were negotiating."

"This is their turf!" Gaia yelled back. "Aren't they going to come after us?"

"No! They're fine! That was a successful business transaction, if you can believe it. Otherwise, believe me, we'd be facedown in a snowdrift!"

Gaia laughed into the wind that whipped across her face, burning her cheeks with both sun and ice. "I don't think Jake knows that!"

Jake was ahead of them. He peered back once in a while to make sure they were still on his tail, but he was in no hurry to slow down. He looked slightly panicked. Gaia felt more alive than she'd felt in a long time.

"That was good," she shot back over her shoulder, after revving the engine a few times and finding a comfortable rate of speed. "I wouldn't have known how to handle all that."

"You pick things up as you go along," Oliver told her. "Some things don't really change. I haven't been in this area in—oh, twenty years, twenty-five? But business is business wherever you go."

"If you call that business," Gaia laughed. "Imagine pulling that at Tower Records."

"We'll try it when we get back."

Gaia grinned into the wind as she steered her snowmobile up into the foothills of the mountains. Oliver really knew his stuff. She was really glad to be on this mission with him, strange as it was to be working with her old enemy—and her father's twin brother. She felt like after years of stagnating, she was learning a million things every second. And even though she was driving the snowmobile, she felt him steering their mission in the right direction. She had made the right decision for once. She was sure of it.

TOM MOORE LAY ON THE ICY-COLD

concrete floor of his cell, meditating deeply. If he concentrated, he could force his body to stop shivering, even though every breath left a puff of vapor above his head. Going even deeper, he felt his consciousness recede until he was nothing but a point of light in a vast darkness. He was in a state of deep, deep trance. From the outside, it looked like he was passed out cold. The awkward position he had put himself in would signal to the guards that he wasn't just having a midday nap. They would have to come in and investigate. Soon, he hoped. Before he froze to death, unprotected and exposed.

Seizur

Vaguely, from a million miles away, he sensed that yes, a guard was slowing outside his cell, peering in to see what was happening. He heard the guard's footsteps fade down the hall, then return with another set of feet. Now two pairs of eyes looked warily into the cell. For a long time. Studying him, seeing if he was faking.

He *was* faking. But they didn't know that.

He heard them whispering back and forth, trying to figure out who to tell and what to do. One of them, the fat one, said they should leave him alone until dinnertime. The other one was afraid he'd die and they would get in trouble for it. Back and forth, back and forth. Finally he willed himself to give a convulsive shudder. It set off a gagging noise in his throat; he hadn't planned it, but it worked wonders. Convinced he was having some sort of seizure, both pairs of boots thumped away down the hall, then returned with medical personnel, who loaded him onto a gurney and wheeled him down to the prison infirmary.

His eyes fluttered open of their own accord, and from his post deep inside his own trance, Tom saw the mountains looming up around him. The prison was in a sort of a basin, set deep inside the mountains. He wasn't even sure which range this was, and even if he had known, he didn't know how he'd survive out there long enough to get to civilization. But this wasn't the time to worry. He had to gather data.

There were probably caves in the mountains. He

could survive in a cave. If he could just overpower these two guards, get outside the compound somehow—but no. This was a fact-finding mission. He had to be patient—wasn't that what he had told Gaia? He had to stick to his plan. A hospital facility was always less guarded than the actual cells. He could catch someone off guard here as they puzzled over his strange comatose state.

"Mr. Moore," a voice called out in accented English. "Mr. Moore. Thomas. Can you hear me?"

I hear you knocking, but you can't come in, Tom thought, willing himself deeper into his trance. He was inside the hospital now; the mountains no longer cradled him. A doctor was the only person near him. If he had to, he could strike out now. He tried to perceive everything going on around him.

It was strange. The doctor didn't seem to be examining him. He had taken a few exploratory probing movements, checked his pupils, but now Tom seemed to be. . . alone? Or was someone standing next to his gurney, eyeing him?

He wanted to look around. This was frustrating. His concentration faltered as he strained to figure out what was going on. Was someone in the room with him? Had they called someone else in? Why was it so quiet? He thought he heard someone breathing. What was—?

He felt the gurney gripped tightly; it gave a sudden lurch, and he felt himself pitched toward the floor.

Instinctively, he sprang up and threw his arms out to break his fall, then rolled to protect himself, ending up in a crouched position, unharmed—but completely awake. Too late, he realized he'd been tricked. Tom Moore looked up to see a smirking doctor in a lab coat shaking his head at him.

"So clumsy," the doctor said, kicking the gurney toward Tom with a violence that seemed out of place with his house-of-healing surroundings.

"Yeah, that gurney seems to be a little wobbly," Tom growled.

"I mean you, Mr. Moore. Your attempt to fool me was quite clumsy. Amateurish, even. I might have expected that sort of foolishness from one of our normal prisoners—the murderers and petty criminals that make up most of our population. From you, it's quite disappointing."

"Why are you keeping me here?" Tom asked. "What kind of criminal am I, according to you?"

"I'd tell you," the doctor said, his smirk deepening until it was infuriatingly smug, "but then I'd have to kill you."

Tom took the invitation and leapt across the room toward the doctor. The two guards went for him immediately. One held him down and the other punched him over and over until the doctor raised a hand to stop them.

"This is hardly what I expected," the doctor said,

more to himself than to Tom. "Very unimpressive indeed. Hold him," he told the guards, and they did, while he injected Tom with something that deadened all thought almost immediately.

"Take him back to his cell," he said, yanking the spike out of Tom's arm with an agonizing twist of his wrist. "He is pathetic. Don't call me again on his behalf. He can die in there for all I care."

In his last moments of consciousness, Tom realized with perfect clarity that he was not going to be able to get out of this place. That even if he did, he would be lost in the white wilderness beyond the walls of the prison. There were no caves he could live in, no path to take; there was nothing but the false bravado he'd used to temporarily deceive himself. But he had lost the strength for self-deception. This wasn't the toughest situation he had ever been in, but it was going to defeat him.

Why? Because it came at a time when he was already emotionally vulnerable. He was worried about Gaia, pining for Natasha, furious at Loki. His only hope now was to steel his mind, rid himself of emotion, and focus on retaining his sanity.

Steel his mind. The mind that was slipping into unconsciousness with terrifying speed.

Steel his—

The apartment on East Seventy-second Street must be the most comfortable place on earth. Except for that terrible couch— the one that Natasha loves so much. That thing is the *least* comfortable place on earth, with its red velvet and mahogany details. But other than that, the apartment is perfect.

I love how Natasha has decorated it. The brick red of the living room is a bold choice, but a good one, and the curtains give it an elegant feel. Too many of those apartments get taken over by families that make them too casual, that don't take into account the grandeur of the good, old building. Natasha understands that. She created a space that acknowledges the beauty of the architecture but is still easy to live in. She can do that, bring together things that seem like they could never meet. It's one of the reasons I fell in love with her.

The girls' room could use some

work—you can see how different their personalities are. Tatiana's a good, kind girl, and her side of the room is as well ordered and tidy as her emotions. But Gaia—well, she's a bit more chaotic. If she'd just do her laundry once in a while. I don't know how she gets any sleep in that bed; it's like she can't get used to the fact that we have a stable environment now. Maybe Tatiana will rub off on her, just a little.

I thought that after Katia died, I'd never feel close to anyone again. The pain of losing her, of losing the warmth and safety of our little three-person society, nearly drove me insane. For months I couldn't even process the simple fact that she was gone. I'd wake up and reach for her. People kept telling me it would get easier, but it didn't. Not really. Once you see true evil you never feel right again. Sometimes you can't get what you want. Sometimes it's ripped from you. And then your heart doesn't just break—it shatters.

Then I met Natasha. She's

fascinating, warm, intelligent—
she's the only woman after Katia
who I've felt I could give my heart
to. The thing that did it for me,
though? The way she opened up to
Gaia. I know how difficult my
daughter can be. And yet Natasha
tried and tried with her, just
because she loved me. Or maybe
because she saw the real girl under
Gaia's shell. Either way, she
earned my eternal respect.

For a few brief hours, I had a
glimpse of how our lives could
entwine together. I saw Natasha
at my side, I saw Gaia relax and
laugh and come as close to happiness as I've seen her since she
was a child. I know—I *know* I
could give her the stability that
was taken away from her. If I
could just protect her and be
there for her, that would give
her the space to feel like a normal kid, a normal teenager. Maybe
she could be happier then. It
wouldn't make up for all the
years I was gone. But it would at
least be something. I'd be her

father again. I just have to get back to her.

Which means getting out of here. This prison. These walls enclosed by mountains wrapped in snow.

Who put me here? Loki. There's no doubt in my mind that the choking fit that led to the blackness from which I awoke here was caused by one person. Not person—entity. Thing with no humanity.

Who ripped me from Natasha? Loki.

Who robbed me of my Gaia yet again? Loki.

And who am I going to make pay for all this pain, when I finally get free?

Loki.

Loki's behind this. But I have a family to get back to, and for them I'll keep my mind steady. But before I return to that comfortable red room, there's one man who's going to pay for his sins in blood so red, it would make the perfect complement to that uncomfortable couch.

Loki.

AS THEY BUZZED UP THROUGH THE

yper

mountains, the darkness moved in around them like a cloak. Oliver finally signaled that they should pull over and meet just under the crest of one of the peaks.

"How are you holding up?" he asked. "Are you tired, or can you keep going?"

"I'm pretty sharp," Gaia said.

"Yeah, this air is keeping me awake," Jake agreed. "Besides, we had so much sleep on the train."

"Good. It'll take the rest of the night for us to travel down the inside of this mountain. Come with me."

They trudged to the top and looked down. "See that ring of lights?" Oliver asked. They nodded. "That's the prison. That's where your father is, Gaia."

Gaia felt a surge of excitement. If she'd been awake before, she was downright hyper now.

"What are we going to do?" she asked.

"We're going to hit it just at dawn. I want you to study the maps I gave you on the train. The two of you are going to sneak into the camp at this location, here, where there's a blind spot that the guards can't see, caused by the rock formations. It's a serious weak spot. I assume they never thought anyone would attempt a rescue."

"They didn't know who they were dealing with, did they?" Jake asked.

"Good," Gaia said. "So we sneak in. Any idea where he's being held?"

"I'm going to guess in here, the innermost tower," Oliver said. "You'll have to figure out a way to enter undetected. Gaia, cover your hair with this cap, and try to walk like a man."

"According to the girls at school, I already do that," she said.

"Well. . . good, then, I suppose. For now." Oliver moved on. "Now, if you're discovered—and chances are you will be—I want you to use this." He pulled out a nasty-looking pistol.

"You need to show me how to use this," Gaia said, eyeing it doubtfully. "I'm not that into guns."

"It's not really a gun. It shoots flares. Shoot it into the air when you want to signal that you're leaving the prison yard. Then Jake can find you at a designated meeting area."

"Is it going to hurt anyone?"

"Not really." Oliver shook his head. Gaia eyed him dubiously.

"Seriously," she said. "Those prisoners have nothing to do with my dad. I don't want them hurt."

"Gaia, I know what you're thinking. This isn't a Loki trick. Just aim the gun toward the sky and no one will get hurt. It's just to get you out of there safely. I promise."

A promise made by an old enemy, now a new friend. It was the best offer Gaia had at the moment. She would have to take it.

"Fine," she said. "Now show me which way to go."

The path shone pale in the deepening twilight. "I'll set up camp here," Oliver said. "We're far enough away that we can rest and let Tom recover if they've mistreated him in any way. Then we can start back."

"Jake should stay," Gaia pointed out. "He's injured. And he shouldn't be on the front lines."

"They'll recognize me," he pointed out. "I'm the exact twin of their most precious prisoner. I can't be seen in there."

"All right." Gaia gazed down the path, toward the lights and barracks that held her father. "I'm ready. Jake, you?"

"I'm good," he said, replacing his goggles. "Oliver, you're sure you'll be okay up here?"

"By the time you get back, I'll practically have a hotel built," he promised. "Get going."

Gaia and Jake slid down the mountain as the darkness gathered. The night would only last a few hours, and they had to hit the prison just before daylight. There was no time to lose.

Dad! Can you hear me? I'm out here.

Shouldn't he be able to tell I'm coming for him? In all those corny TV movies, fathers and daughters seem to know everything about each other with one wink. They sense all sorts of things, as if a telephone wire connects them at the heart.

Then again, in all those Shakespeare plays, the daughter dresses like a boy and her dad doesn't realize it's her. I don't know what kind of dumb dads were running around in the seventeenth century, but it's right there in the plays. So maybe he can't tell I'm coming. Maybe with my hair under this watch cap, he won't know it's me. I'll be like Viola or Rosalind, and in the end I'll get everything I want.

I think I can see the rock for- mation Oliver was talking about. Off to the side there—yeah. The maps were really good. I don't know how he did it. Must have

been satellite photos or something.

I can't believe it, but everything he comes up with keeps
checking out. No matter how suspicious I am of him—and I'm not
sure I'll ever be one hundred
percent convinced of his
sincerity—he keeps coming
through. I couldn't have gotten
this far without him. And now I'm
within spitting distance of my
dad. It's so odd. But no odder
than the plot of a play where
twins end up finding each other
on the streets of Verona, thirty
years after they lost each other
at sea. I guess stranger things
have happened.

Of course, that was fiction.

AS INSTRUCTED, GAIA AND JAKE

parked their snowmobiles. Under the cover of darkness they built a makeshift fort to camouflage the vehicles and keep them protected. It took a while, and Gaia could feel

Riot

the darkness starting to wane, hinting at gray around the edges.

"Are you ready for this?" she asked Jake.

"Yeah. I'm going to go in there and set off a series of explosions. The guards are going to assume they came from some of the inmates trying to cause a distraction so they can escape."

"You've got those fireworks?" Gaia asked.

"I've got everything, and it's all still dry. With any luck, the guards will be so disorganized, they'll split up in too many directions to notice us," Jake said as he dug a stake into the ground to anchor the fort.

"Right. And the inmates—they'll either start fighting amongst themselves or take advantage of the confusion to try to escape themselves." Gaia kicked her stake to make sure it was stable.

"And that's when we bust your dad out."

Gaia grinned. "Yeah. That's when we bust my dad out."

"You excited?"

"What do you think?" Gaia packed away her grin and gave a deep breath. "Okay. Let's do this thing."

Jake nodded. Gaia could just make out the outline

of his head in the inky blackness. Together they used their Oliver-issued night-vision goggles to find their way through the snow to the rocky outcropping that would give them access to the prison. They entered easily. Just as Oliver had told them, there was a fissure in the wall that gave them access to the main yard. Gaia ran across the yard to the tower.

Her heart raced as she entered the building. She knew she was close. She could sense her father's presence. She entered the building and ran up the dank stairs. He was sure to be at the top; that was the most difficult place to escape from, because it could be seen from everywhere in the prison.

Rounding the last flight, she saw a cell at the end of a hallway. Inside it was a figure in a gray uniform, head bowed. It couldn't be so easy. But apparently it was. There, right before her eyes—

"Dad!"

The head came up. In an instant, Gaia saw the face that was so much like Oliver's, but now instantly recognizable as her father's. She had found him. After what seemed like a lifetime of wondering, thousands of miles crossed, and an immeasurable amount of worry, she'd found him. Her father, Tom Moore. Her heart bloomed in her chest till it almost choked her with emotion.

Except something was wrong.

"Dad?"

Yes, technically, Gaia was standing in front of her father, Tom Moore. But he didn't know it yet. Gaia's heart broke when she saw what had been done to him. He'd been beaten, she could see that immediately. But there was something worse. He looked defeated, and he blinked at her as though he thought he might be hallucinating.

"I wish you were real," he said in a low voice.

The words pressed into her heart like a red-hot cattle brand. He didn't even recognize that she was real? What was going on?

"I *am* real, Dad! It's me!"

Forcing herself to act instead of worry, she ran forward and yanked on the door. She jimmied a crowbar between the bars and snapped them open, reaching through to grab him and break through whatever dream state he was in.

"Dad," she said.

His eyes peered out at her, red-rimmed and haggard. She shook his collar. He jerked back, as though he hadn't expected her to actually reach out and touch him. To Gaia, it felt like she'd been slapped. She threw her arms around him and squeezed.

"Come back," she begged. "Come back. It's me. It's Gaia. I'm really here." Her voice broke and she fought back tears. "Dad, don't do this." She pulled back, smoothing her hands across his face. He studied her with a puzzled expression.

"Come on," she moaned. "Hey!" She shook him a

little. Finally, his eyes widened. A spark entered them. Relief flooded Gaia's veins as their eyes connected for real.

"Gaia," he said, his voice husky and harsh. He hugged her back, crushing her in a desperate embrace. She waited to hear him say something, ask how she got there, tell her he loved her.

"*Behind you,*" he whispered. Without needing to think before she reacted, Gaia turned with her foot already in the air and caught a guard straight in the gut. The guy fell backward into his partner, who ran yelling down the stairs.

"*Jake!*" she shouted, knowing he was just outside in the yard. In response, she heard a whoosh and a pop, then smelled acrid smoke. Immediately, shouts filled the courtyard.

The prison riot was on.

Wiping out
at seventy-
five miles
per hour
would turn **nerve**
them both
into **endings**
red smudges
in the white
snow.

TOM MOORE WATCHED IN AMAZEMENT

Face-to-Face

as he realized his hallucination was real. His daughter was here; she had appeared out of nowhere, as if his mind had created her out of the raw material around him. She beat both guards, the ones who had beaten him, and then she turned around to where he was standing, still, in the opened prison cell.

"Dad. *Dad*. Come on. We've got to go."

"I'm groggy," he explained. "Some sort of drug. Knocked me out."

"Well, the air's cold enough to wake you up." She took off her own coat and put it on him. He followed her out.

"How?" he asked. "I can't figure out how."

"I'll explain later. Right now, we've just got to get out of here."

They hurried down the stairs. Tom felt like an old man. He was trained to handle harsh conditions, but this prison had been the most brutal place he'd ever experienced. Even in the short time he'd been here, the cold had sunk into his muscles, robbing them of strength. He'd barely been fed at all. And his lungs felt weak. He was embarrassed to be seen like this.

At the bottom of the stairs, he stopped Gaia. "Be careful," he said. "Those guards have a supervisor, a doctor. He's a brutal man—and he has some sort of interest in keeping me here."

"I'll watch for him. Right now, we need to head across the yard there. Do you see where we got in? There was a fault in the wall and we broke through."

The yard looked like a scene from a war movie. Men dressed in the thick, burlaplike uniform of the prison had broken en masse from their barracks, panicked by the acrid smoke, and were running in all different directions. Tom could see that a group of them had ganged up on some of the guards, repaying them in kind for the cruelty they'd been shown. There were fistfights going on all around them, and bricks were flying through the air like concrete-colored missiles. It was hard to see through the smoke and chaos. But the noise helped jar him out of his grogginess and his mind started to focus.

"I see it," answered Tom.

"I need to find Jake in all this mess. Wow."

"We can't look for your friend now," he said. "We need to get out of here ourselves. If you planned this properly, he'll know to meet us on the outside if we can't be found."

"Hang on," Gaia said, scanning the early dawn sky. Was she waiting for a helicopter? Tom didn't see how that would work. Where would it land? Suddenly there was a loud popping sound, and a flare shot up into the air. Gaia's eyes followed it to its source and she grinned.

"I can't believe that worked," Gaia said, shoving Tom

in the direction of the exit. For the next few moments, he knew nothing but the need to run, as he avoided flying fists, bricks, and even bodies. A few others had found the broken wall and were piling out. They only had a few moments before the guards discovered it, too, and began shooting at anyone trying to escape.

Once outside the walls, they ran straight toward the woods, where they were joined by a young man Tom didn't know. "You did this?" he asked the boy. "You're Gaia's age. How did this happen? What's going on?"

"Nice to meet you, Mr. Moore," the young man said. "I'm Jake Montone." He turned to Gaia. "We need to get the snowmobiles and get back to Oliver. I don't like how this thing is going down," Jake said, as he departed for the makeshift fort.

"Oliver?" Tom gasped. He wheeled around, yanking his arm out of Gaia's grasp. "Please don't tell me you're working with my brother. Is that who brought you here?"

Gaia looked at her father, horrified that Jake had let the secret slip so soon. He would have had to find out sooner or later, but she'd thought she'd have the trip up the mountain to soften the blow. "Dad, this isn't the time. Let's just get up the—"

"What kind of a deal did you make? Do you have any idea how much danger we are in right now?"

"Yeah, Dad. There's a riot going on and—you hear that? Those are gunshots. We need to get on the snow-mobiles now."

"I'm safer inside that compound than out here with Loki. He's using you, can't you see that? He must have lost control of my abduction, and he used to you get me back—now he's going to kill all of us."

"It's not like that," Gaia shouted over the increasing noise of the riot. "He was in a coma. He had some kind of brain conversion while he was under. Sometimes when people suffer loss of oxygen to the brain they emerge from their comas a gentler version of their former selves. In this case, Loki just went back to his Oliver personality. He helped us put this trip together—he put it together for us. Dad, I know it's hard to believe, but he's really sorry."

"Sorry?" Tom asked, with an incredulous stare at his daughter. She almost withered under its heat. He didn't raise his voice, but his body language was unmistakable. He was furious.

Jake buzzed up on a snowmobile. "Is everything all right?" he asked. "Mr. Moore, can you ride on the back of this with me?"

Tom turned to Jake. "Thank you for your help—but my daughter and I aren't going with you."

"What? Dad!" Gaia said.

"There's no way you'll get back without the snowmobiles," Jake said. "And the rations. And the supplies."

"We'll manage," Tom said, taking Gaia's arm protectively.

"Dad, listen," Gaia said. She turned to face him.

"Jake's right. We're dead meat on our own. Even if you're still suspicious of Oliver, you've got to trust me enough to know we'll be all right. If we go with him, maybe something will happen. But if we don't, there's no chance of survival. And there's no turning back," she added, with a toss of her head toward the now-mounting flames inside the prison walls.

Tom gazed into Gaia's eyes as if he were trying to gauge whether she'd been brainwashed or not. It was a legitimate question. Loki had been a master of manipulation—Tom himself had been fooled by Gaia doppelgangers, though not from this close up. But there was no time to think it over carefully. He had to act quickly.

"Sir?" Jake asked. "If one of those bullets hits my gas tank, we're going to have some trouble."

"All right," he said. "I'll go with you." He climbed on the back of the kid's snowmobile while Gaia buzzed on ahead. She was right. He had no choice—for now. But he was going to watch carefully for a chance to grab his daughter and get away from Loki. Or use this opportunity to get revenge.

He didn't know what Loki was up to now, but he was about to come face-to-face with his old nemesis. What did Loki want? What was his plan? Tom wasn't sure. But he knew that, bottom line, it had to be evil. And being this close to Loki was going to give Tom the opportunity for revenge he'd always wanted. The temptation was beyond unbearable.

I don't think I could be more
worried if Gaia were actually my
own daughter. I've been watching
since I finished setting up camp.
Everything is in order. The food
is ready, the coffee is brewing.
Now all I can do is watch from my
perch up here on the mountain.
Gaia's down there somewhere, and
she's with my brother.

My brother. How am I going to
face him?

Tom has every right to detest
me with all his heart. I ruined
his life—and even tried to take
it. I nearly destroyed Gaia time
and time again. I have been behind
every painful betrayal of the last
five years, and there have been
many of them. Too many to count.
Too many to remember. The flashes
that come to me nearly drive me
insane with regret and remorse. A
lifetime of penance couldn't make
up for what I did.

Still, here I am. I brought
Gaia to him, and I'm going to
carry him out of here on my back

if I have to. It's the least I can
do. I owe him that much. After
that, if he still wants to hate
me, I can't stop him. But at least
I can prove to him that I can be
trusted with this one task.

I can hear shouts and gunshots.
The prison is boiling with rioting
prisoners. I saw the flare, so I
know Gaia found her father. Did
they get out? If I see two snowmobiles climbing toward me—and I
think I do—then they did.

The shouts. The gunshots. The
prisoners are rioting. Why am I
drawn to the sound? Is it familiar? Is there something I don't
remember from my Loki years that
is being set off now? The sound
is so familiar—

It's like there are two of me.
As I gaze down the mountain, I'm
horrified by the danger and chaos
in that prison. But I worry. Is
Loki still alive inside me? Is he
relishing the shouts? Does the
clamor sound as pleasant as the
laughter of children to him? If
he's here, I can't sense him. But

I'm worried that I will. If he
appears out of my subconscious,
I'll have to lock him up, keep
him out of my way.

Concentrate on the pain, the horror of it, the worry about Gaia and
Tom. If I can keep that fresh, I can
remain myself and keep them safe
from him. From that part of me.

Hurry up, Gaia. Get Tom up here
so I can see him safe. So I can
apologize like a man. This is the
most terrifying thing I've ever
had to do—not because I'm afraid
he'll harm me, but because I have
to admit what I became, what I
was. What might still be, deep
inside. Facing Tom will be the
hardest thing I've ever had to do.

And I'd just as soon get it
over with.

Hurry up, Gaia.

GAIA PULLED UP FIRST. SHE JUMPED

Hostility

off the snowmobile and ran to Oliver.

"He's not doing so great," she said.

"Was he injured?"

She grimaced. "I mean, he's a little wasted. He doesn't look so hot. But that's not the problem."

Oliver looked up at her, curious.

"It's going to be really hard for me to convince him you're trustworthy," she blurted out.

"Well, of course. We expected that." Oliver returned to his food-preparation activities, stirring a pot of beans carefully. Gaia watched him. He was nervous, anyone could tell.

"I guess I just thought he'd have more faith in me," she said quietly.

Oliver looked up at her. "Gaia, your father and I were bitter enemies for most of your life. You can't erase that in a few days. Don't expect too much of him right now. This is a huge shock. And it's not the only shock he's going to have to deal with. Don't forget, he has no idea that Natasha and Tatiana turned against him. This is going to be quite a blow."

Gaia breathed in sharply. She knew she was going to have to deliver that news, too. This was just getting harder and harder. She'd finally gotten what she wanted—she had found her father and delivered him

129

from prison—and she felt almost nothing but nerve endings.

Jake buzzed up behind Gaia in his snowmobile and pulled it up right next to hers. He was completely casual about it, like he was pulling into a parking spot at the mall. Gaia had to smile. The guy handled himself like a pro.

"Hey!" She plastered on a smile and ran toward Jake and Tom. "Come on over. There's food. . . ."

Tom climbed off the back of the snowmobile and stalked over to Oliver. She could see that his eyes were aflame with fury. "Dad, come on," she said. But he walked past her as if she wasn't even there. Oliver put the metal pot down on the fire and moved away from the flames, instinctively taking himself away from the vulnerable situation. Tom grabbed him by the collar and shook him furiously. The weakness brought on by his imprisonment was gone. Empowered by his anger, Tom was suddenly a tower of strength, lunging at his brother full force.

"What's your game?" he asked, grabbing Oliver by the collar.

"I know this is strange," Oliver told him, hands in the air. "I'm not here to hurt you."

"Do I look like an idiot?" Tom asked, shoving Oliver backward. "Do you think I'm a fool? You expect me to eat food you prepared? So you can poison me again? You've done enough. I don't know why you're pretending to help me or how you've fooled Gaia, but

I'm not falling for it. Go. Get out of here. Find your own way back to civilization."

Tom punctuated his tirade with little jabs at Oliver's chest. Oliver stepped backward slowly, absorbing the blows, hands in the air in surrender. Finally Tom gave him a shove and he tripped, falling backward into the snow.

"Out of here," Tom repeated. "Take a snowmobile and go."

"Dad, stop!" Gaia shouted.

"Tom. Listen," Oliver said, getting up and standing at a wary distance. "I'm not going to fight you. You need me to get out of here."

"I need you for nothing," Tom screamed. "You want to help me? Bring my wife back."

Oliver winced as if he'd just been pushed again. "I'm so sorry," he said.

"Sorry about what? About killing my wife?" Tom asked.

"That wasn't *me*."

"No, it was Loki. And Loki is who, exactly?"

Oliver bowed his head in shame.

"I'm not hearing an answer. Who is Loki?"

"He's me. He *was* me. Loki was me, but I'm not him anymore. You have to believe me."

Tom reached for the handle of the pot on the fire, ready to swing it at Oliver and let the boiling soup and the heavy iron finish him off. Gaia stepped in, using techniques she had learned from Tom himself to paralyze him momentarily.

"That's enough," she said. "Dad, you and I are going to sit over here. Oliver and Jake will build a new fire. Right?"

Oliver nodded. Jake looked dubious.

"Come on, Dad, sit down. Come on." Tom allowed himself to be led to the fire and sat down. Gaia crouched next to him for a moment, putting her arms around his shoulders. She suddenly felt very protective of him. She'd rescued him, but he wasn't out of the woods yet— literally or figuratively.

"This is a lot to take in," she said. "Maybe you're right, and maybe I'm just being an idiot about Oliver. But we're okay for now. Just hang in there with me."

Tom nodded. Gaia got up and went to Oliver and Jake, who were already busy setting up their alternate camp.

"Oliver," she said. "This is weird. I mean, it's awkward. You've been so great, but—"

"Your father is showing me the same suspicion you did," Oliver acknowledged. "It's understandable. Be patient with him."

"Oh, I am," she said. "I just hope you will be, too."

Oliver nodded, giving Gaia a reassuring smile.

"I think it's also the imprisonment—the torture. His mind isn't quite working at full capacity. He told me they pumped him full of all kinds of drugs. He doesn't even know what they are."

"And without a laboratory, we don't know, either," Oliver said. "So I'm up against Tom's legitimate suspicions plus his lowered capacity to be reasonable. The trip back to New York should be quite interesting."

"Well. . . I guess it'll be like any other dysfunctional family reunion," Gaia said.

She looked toward Jake. He seemed freaked out. She didn't even know what to say to him. As far as he knew, Oliver was a great guy who'd been helping them. He didn't really know Gaia's long history with Loki, just the broad strokes. She couldn't risk telling Jake any more than that. In this case, too much information could be a dangerous thing. Now, though, she wished she'd prepared him for how scary Loki was. Just to give him some perspective. She suddenly felt a wave of guilt for having let him come along. For not having let him make an informed decision.

But she couldn't worry about that now. Her priority was Tom. Her dad. He wasn't doing so great. She had to nurse him back to health—and get the last of those drugs out of his system so he could return to his normal self.

She tromped back over to the Gaia-and-Tom fire and sat down on a folding camp chair next to his, in the shelter Oliver had constructed. "So we'll rest here, then go to Moscow and get the plane back to the U.S.," she said.

Tom gazed at his daughter. The grizzle of his unshaven face made him look older than he was, older than his brother. The red rims of his eyes could have been the result of sadness or illness—it was hard to tell. Finally he nodded.

"How's the food?"

He looked down at the bowl of beans in his hands. "I haven't been able to bring myself to eat it."

"You need your strength," Gaia said gently. "Here, look." She dipped a spoon into it and brought it to her mouth. "Ow! It's hot. But it's fine."

Tom nodded again and took the spoon back from Gaia. She wrapped him in a blanket that looked like tinfoil and rubbed his shoulders. She hated seeing him like this.

She was suddenly ravenous, and tucked into her own bowl of food with an enthusiasm she hadn't known she had. She wanted to get the meal over with and get moving. At least with the buzz of the snowmobiles in her ear, she wouldn't have to listen to the uncomfortable silence between her father and her uncle.

"This is kind of good," she said.

"Probably because we're so hungry," he answered. "Gaia, thank you. Whatever else is going on, I can't believe you made it all this way. I thought I was lost in there."

"I couldn't sleep till I found you," she told him. "There was no way."

"Do I really look that bad?"

Gaia laughed. "You've looked better, I guess. Do you think you can drive?"

"I'd be happy to."

"Good. I'll ride with you, Jake will ride with—on the other one. Okay?"

"Fine."

They sipped in silence again.

"The game plan," she finally told him, "is that we're going to travel back on the train, but instead of being passengers, we'll hop on the freight cars this time."

"Sounds wise," he said. "That's a good plan."

Gaia's heart skipped a beat. *Funny how your dad's approval always gives you that warm feeling*, she thought. *Even when you just had to bust him out of jail.*

She wanted to get going. Get out of this odd isolated location, with this odd group. Funny how all the easiness of the last few days had vanished. She hoped her dad would come around soon, before she developed an ulcer from all this hostility.

Maybe it's a dysfunctional family, Gaia thought, *but it's my dysfunctional family.*

Okay, I found my dad. I haven't had a second to process all of this. Here I am, riding down the side of a mountain behind him, hanging on to him for dear life. I've been hugging him for hours, but I still don't feel like I really have him back.

Maybe there's only so many times you can lose someone and get them back. Maybe after a certain number of times, your heart says, "Enough. I'm not going up and down anymore."

Or maybe he doesn't seem like my dad. My dad is physically strong and incredibly sharp-witted. Even when he's angry, he doesn't let his emotions get away with him. He should be able to deal with Oliver, even if he thinks he's secretly still Loki, until we get back to New York. And he should be able to see that I've assessed Oliver and trust my judgment about him.

I mean, I'm not an idiot. I understand my dad's point. When

Oliver was Loki, he was absolute undiluted evil. Caused us pain beyond measure. Hurt people thoughtlessly. Almost for the sport of it.

But I've checked him out. And I believe he's changed. And if I can investigate him and come to that conclusion, Dad should trust my instincts.

Then again. . . then again, maybe I *am* wrong, and Dad's right. I mean, we both trusted George Niven. He was Dad's oldest friend, the person he'd left me with to take care of me, and neither one of us could tell he'd hooked up with a wife who was trying to kill me. And then there was George himself. He got Dad captured in the Caribbean.

And me? Everything I believed in has fallen apart. I thought I could trust Natasha and Tatiana, until I found the gun used to shoot at me hidden in the very same bedroom I shared with the little creep. So maybe I'm not as smart as I thought.

This is complicated, but I have to go with the plan. Unless Oliver shows some reason for me to stop trusting him as much as I have, I have to let him guide us home. That's how missions like this work. I have to take care of my dad, get him healthy, and hope his emotional outbursts go away as the drugs leach out of his system. And I have to follow Oliver's lead.

Thank goodness I have my dad back. He's reminding me to think critically about everything and everyone. Maybe when we're on the train, I'll have a chance to talk to him—really talk this through and fill him in on how Oliver's been acting. Maybe together we can figure out how much to trust him.

Because right now, I want to. And this is one thing I really don't want to be wrong about.

I'm guiding this snowmobile across the frozen tundra, with my daughter on the back. The air is cold and refreshing. The snow is bright and sharp. But I don't feel right. I do not feel right at all.

Part of it is physical. The buzzing in my ears? It could just as easily be the snowmobile's engine—or it could be an internal ringing, the siren song that hits just before unconsciousness. I shouldn't be driving this thing. But I can't admit to Gaia how sick I still feel.

Yes, the food was nourishing and good. But I took many beat-ings in the short time I was in that prison. And those drugs. . . whatever they were, they've diminished my capacity to react reasonably. They are clouding my judgment. I'm useless as a father right now. Useless as an agent.

But if Loki finds out how diminished my abilities are, he's sure to strike—sooner than he'd

planned. At least this way, if I
fake feeling relatively healthy,
I can buy enough time to get back
to normal.

Focus, Tom. Focus hard.
Everything rides on your ability
to steer this snowmobile—and this
mission—as much as you can.

Then again, I have to confront
the possibility that Gaia trusted
Oliver for a reason. I raised her
to have a critical mind. And Loki
has given her enough reason to
hate him for life. She's certainly not naïve, nor is she nat-
urally trusting in any way. Maybe
she sensed something in him that
has really changed.

Difficult as it might be to
believe, I have to accept that
possibility. I'm an agent, after
all; I'm supposed to be able to
consider any possibility, no matter how unlikely.

What a concept. My brother,
Oliver. . . could be my brother,
Oliver, once again. I buried him
years ago, deep in my heart,
accepting and mourning him as

-

dead. Because he was dead to me. Now, the idea that he might be resurrected. . . I don't know what to do about that. Right now, I can't even process it. I can't admit to myself how much I have missed my brother over these years, and how fantastic it would be to have him back.

My God, what if what Gaia says is true? What if Oliver is back from the dead, and Loki is really gone?

I can't focus on that now. I have to keep my defenses up as much as possible. I have to work to control my emotions. I have to fight to keep my mind focused and functional. And I have to appear much healthier than I feel.

It's a tall order. But I've fought tougher battles. And won.

I'll win this one, too.

I just hope that hum is the snowmobile after all.

GAIA PICKED HER HEAD UP AND

Steel Whee

peered down the mountain. In the distance she could see the railway yard. The trains were lined up, ready to rejoin the regular rails and return to Moscow. They could hop on one easily, if they could figure out which was the next to go. Otherwise they'd have to wait till one moved, then board while it was still rolling slowly. That was less safe, but surer. She tucked her head back into the wind-free zone behind her father's back. They were still a long way away; it would be a while before they got there. She tried to calculate in her head how fast they'd have to move and how much time they'd have to get on the train, mentally rehearsing the moves she'd have to use, flexing her muscles to keep them warm.

Gaia relaxed as much as she could on the back of the snowmobile. It wasn't as cozy as the train car. For one thing, the wind was freezing wherever her skin was exposed, and she had to keep shifting so she wouldn't get frostbite. Not to mention that this was a snowmobile, not an upholstered couch on steel wheels: She couldn't exactly lean back and have a snooze. But the steady buzzing of the engine and the smooth sailing of the journey were enough to lull her into a state of calm.

Until she sensed something strange. Like when she

was riding the subway and it took on too much speed. Or when she was in an old elevator and it dipped unexpectedly before stopping at a floor. She picked her head up again. She could see Oliver and Jake up ahead, on the right, and she squeezed her father's arm to make sure he saw them, too.

She felt a distressing lack of response. Something was wrong.

She shook Tom's shoulders and felt the snowmobile waver in response. She couldn't even tell if he was conscious or not. But it was clear something was going drastically wrong. Gaia clung to him for dear life as the snowmobile skipped over the snow at a ludicrous speed. Wiping out at seventy-five miles per hour would turn them both into red smudges in the white snow.

She had to get it under control—and fast!

Tom and Oliver, identical in every way, sat on opposite sides of the **which one?** fire, both glaring into the flames.

GAIA POUNDED ON HER FATHER'S

Peculiar

back, trying to wake him from whatever stupor he was in as they sped across the snowy plane. Her fists bounced off him like pebbles, he was so steely and tense. She shouted at him, then reached as far forward as she could and grabbed the handlebars of the snowmobile. It was tough—she could barely reach—but if she shoved herself forward, she could just get a handhold. She tried to squeeze down on the hand brakes. The bike slowed, but wobbled again because her balance was off. Gaia let go and they sped up again.

To make matters worse, they had almost caught up to Oliver and Jake. The two of them were looking back curiously. She tried to shout to them to keep away— that she was out of control—but the words were whipped out of her mouth by the wind. She just prayed they'd steer clear—literally.

The next step was going to be tricky. She could lose a leg if they landed wrong. But if it was her leg versus all four of them in a midsnow collision, she'd have to make the sacrifice. It was a gamble she had to take.

This was where having no fear came in handy. She knew pain might be coming, but that didn't stop her from doing what she had to do.

Gaia wrenched the steering mechanism to the left,

yanking herself and Tom off course and causing a sickening lurch. The snowmobile, like a puzzled horse, tried to stay on course, but the sudden change of direction threw it completely out of control. Gaia pushed forward so she'd be flung back when the snowmobile crashed, which it did almost immediately. She landed on the icy crust of snow with a brutal crack. Tom landed facedown and spread-eagle, like a snow angel, and the snowmobile spun wildly a few times, then lay on its side, still buzzing, then shorting out and stalling with a hopeless cough.

It was a good thing they were close enough to the railway, because the snowmobile was dead.

Oliver and Jake pulled up immediately. Oliver hopped off and ran over, first pulling Gaia to a sitting position.

"Gaia! Are you all right?" he asked. "My God, what happened? Did you lose control?"

"Uh. . . I don't know," she said, thinking fast. Had her dad tried to kill Oliver in a fit of drug-induced rage? Had he briefly lost consciousness? Was he sicker than she realized? Whatever the case, it wouldn't be smart to let Oliver know there was any weakness at all. Just in case there was more Loki in him than she thought.

"Get Dad," she said. "Here, let me." She stood, wincing in pain at the wrenched feeling in her leg, and ran over to him. She flipped him over on his back and was relieved to see him blink up at the darkening sky. He turned his head toward her.

"Your nose," he said. "You're bleeding."

Oh, crap. She swiped the blood away and tilted her head back.

"I'm fine," she said. "The snowmobile lost control. Right, Dad?"

She peered down at him sidewise, hoping he'd play along.

It took him a moment longer than it should have, but his mind clicked into sync with hers.

"It lost control," he agreed. "Damn thing must be fifteen, twenty years old."

"Well, at least it got us here," Oliver said. "I'm glad you're all right."

Jake looked at Tom curiously, but he was busying himself taking care of Gaia's nose.

"What happened?" she hissed up at Tom.

"I'm not sure," he said. "I think I lost consciousness."

"Is that really what happened?"

They stared at each other, wary. Gaia wasn't sure if her dad was all the way back from his drug- and prison-induced weakness yet. Tom wasn't sure he could—or should—admit to her how weak he really was. So the silence blossomed between them, replete with the aroma of distrust.

But they were father and daughter, after all. The

moment passed, and they stood up, trudging behind Jake and Oliver toward the rail yard.

Since they couldn't actually enter until well after nightfall, they set up camp in the woods at the edge of the plain, in view of the railway yard but far enough away that they wouldn't seem suspicious. They set the temporary shelter up, all vinyl and space-age metal rods. It was surprisingly comfortable, creating a little igloo of warmth. They built a fire, creating a ring of wood to house the unlikely element of heat in the frozen tundra. Oliver unpacked more of the aluminum foil–style blankets.

"I'll never understand how these work," Gaia said. "They're warmer than fur."

"They used to sleep under shiny metal blankets on *Star Trek*," Jake pointed out. "I knew that show was ahead of its time. It always looked kind of uncomfortable, but now I get it."

Gaia smiled at him gratefully. Okay, so things wouldn't be as easygoing as they'd been on the train ride up to the prison. But if she could just get everyone talking, maybe she could reevaluate Oliver's trustworthiness—and assess how incapacitated Tom was.

It seemed impossible, though. Tom and Oliver, identical in every way, sat on opposite sides of the fire, both glaring into the flames like they were waiting for a phoenix to hoist itself up and into the sky. Their low-slung camping chairs sagged, not just under their weight, but under the weight of their respective bad feelings. Tom had pounds of suspicion, and Oliver, it seemed, had pounds of guilt.

Gaia spread a blanket on the ground and sat between them, facing the fire. If her dad was high noon, her uncle was 6 P.M., and she was three o'clock. Time for a truce — of sorts.

Jake sat down next to her. With a rush she realized she'd barely spoken to him in the last twenty-four hours or longer. It was strange—she'd missed him. And she wanted to talk to him now. To explain the strange tension between her father and Oliver. From his point of view, her dad was probably just a peculiar, scattered, ungrateful jerk. If you didn't know he was shot full of sedatives, and that Loki was a seriously evil overlord who had taken over Oliver's consciousness for the better part of the last twenty years, you might have thought that.

But this was no time for an intimate tête-à-tête. She had to play ambassador.

She cleared her throat. "So, did I mention that my dad and my uncle are twins?" Gaia asked. Ostensibly she was talking to Jake, but she said it loud enough for everyone to hear. "My—my mom used to tell me that when they were kids, they dressed alike. Not by choice. She said their mom made them. Their mom had a picture with both of them in sailor outfits. She couldn't even tell which was which, they looked so similar. It always cracked her up."

"Sailor outfits," Jake said, playing along. "I didn't know they really made those."

"I saw the picture when I was a kid. It was pretty funny. Dorky. Extremely dorky."

A silence so loud it seemed to scream settled over the campfire. It crackled hopefully, but neither man said a word.

"My dad was kind of a nerd," Gaia said. "They both went to Columbia University."

"Oh, my dad's dying for me to go there," Jake said.

"I couldn't stand those sailor suits," Tom muttered, staring into the flames. He didn't sound angry. But he didn't sound exactly friendly, either. "I put mine on to make Mother happy, but I did feel extremely. . . dorky."

"I didn't mind," Oliver said. "It was clean and white. That appealed to me."

The two of them were addressing their comments to the fire, not to each other.

"Yes," Tom added after a pause. "Oliver did like things neat. His side of the room was always well ordered and tidy."

"And Tom made a point of not being neat," Oliver said. "Right after that photo was taken, he ran off into the woods. Came back so covered in dirt, bark, and sap, the suit would never get clean again. Mother had no choice but to throw it out. That was the end of our naval careers."

Gaia gave a snorting laugh, which set her nose bleeding again. She had to tilt her head back, pack snow on it, and lean against Jake. Which almost made it pleasant.

"So you stopped dressing alike?" she asked.

"Yes," Oliver said.

"No, not really," Tom disagreed. "We had a lot of the same clothes. You just couldn't tell because mine were always several shades darker than his."

"Hah." Gaia gave a less snorty laugh.

Silence blew in again, but a less uncomfortable version this time. Gaia watched the two men. They weren't looking at each other, but their conversation—stilted, not quite easy, but a few sentences of conversation nonetheless—had limped along with nobody punching anybody else. They'd even shared a little family memory. Okay, so they weren't exactly skipping down memory lane together. But this was a step in the right direction.

She stared into the flames, skootching a bit closer so that the heat enveloped her. The blanket reflected the heat back onto her, and the one around her shoulders kept it next to her skin; it was very, very cozy.

She knew she should take this moment to tell her father about Natasha. The longer she waited, the harder it would be. She stared at the flames licking at the wood and dancing up and down. This was so nice. Like being next to a fireplace.

This was the first time Tom had relaxed since the rescue, she told herself. She didn't want to shatter his calm. Obviously this particular imprisonment had been harder for him than most of his adventures. Maybe it was the drugs, maybe he was getting older. Maybe it was because he'd only escaped another prison two weeks before and hadn't quite gotten over that one. But if she told him about Natasha, she'd make it worse. Better to let him gather some strength before giving him more bad news.

She'd tell him later.

JAKE WATCHED GAIA DROWSING BY

the fire. For the first time, he was hit by the full oddity of this situation. He was a high school student from Manhattan who'd had his eye on an interesting-looking girl. And now he was in the middle of nowhere on another continent, looking at that same girl, who had

Weapon of Mass Destructio

turned out to be more interesting than anyone had a right to be. It was nuts.

Gaia's head gave that falling-asleep nod, then jerked back up. Her eyes darted left and right, to make sure her dad and her uncle hadn't seen. Then she pulled her knees up to her chin and rested her head there, looking into the flames again. Something dangerous was happening here. Jake sensed that. Dangerous in a different way from the bricks being flung at him or bullets grazing his shoulder. Something about the way Gaia pulled her cap down over her forehead, or stared into the flames, or scratched her nose (angrily, like it pissed her off by itching) gave Jake the feeling that she could destroy him more completely than any weapon of mass destruction. He was falling in love. At least, he thought he was. With Gaia. And that seemed more perilous than any of the other stuff.

Her head slid off her knees and she pulled them up more tightly, still not able to get comfortable. Jake knew that the safe thing would be to stay right where he was, maybe organize some of their camping gear a little better or scrape out some extra food from a pot. But the safe thing had never appealed to him. He walked over to Gaia and sat down on her blanket, leg-to-leg and hip-to-hip. Gaia didn't give him a look. She didn't give him a wisecrack. She just, miraculously, laid her head on his shoulder, without a word.

Jake sat rigidly, not sure what to do. He couldn't think of anything to say. He didn't want to ruin the moment—if it *was* a moment. Was it a moment? Was he having a moment with Gaia Moore? Now it was his turn to look back and forth from her dad to her uncle. All he wanted to do was put an arm around her shoulder. No, if he was going to be honest about it, what he wanted to do was lay her on her side and curl his body around her, keeping her warm and—for a few minutes, anyway— safe. Not that she wanted saving, but somehow that only made it even more imperative that he take care of her.

But talk about dangerous: She basically had two dads who could kick Jake's ass in a heartbeat. Not to mention that she could, too. His arm stayed where it was.

"How are you doing?" he finally murmured in a low voice. He was answered with a long, slow snore.

"Oh. That's good," he answered.

He tried to listen in on Oliver and Tom's conversation, still droning on over his head. But the campfire was awfully warm. Plus there was Gaia's body heat. And the comfort of being so close to her. It was pretty irresistible.

Funny how anyplace could feel cozy if you were with the right company, he thought.

And then he was asleep, too.

THE PIERCING BLAST OF A TRAIN

A Dad-Sized Arm

whistle jolted Gaia and Jake awake. They both sat up, blinking, realizing they'd been pretty much curled up together. Gaia also realized she'd been drooling.

"Ugh. Sorry," she said. "My head feels like a science experiment. What's going on?"

The sky was a deep violet color, almost black; the only lights were the ones from the rail yard. It had to be three in the morning. The fire was gone, stamped out and covered in snow by Oliver, while Tom was packing away the last of their camping equipment, except for the blankets Gaia and Jake were using.

"Give me those," he said. "Are you awake? Sorry, I know it's late."

"No, I'm fine." Gaia stood and folded one of the blankets. Jake folded the other one. Then he took some snow and rubbed it across his face.

"Man, I was really out," he said.

"Shake a leg," Oliver said, handing one of them a pack. "Come on, that's our train right there. It should be coming past us in a few minutes."

The train chugged out of the railway yard, moving toward them slowly. But as it got closer, Gaia saw that it was going faster than it had seemed. The four of them started running at top speed. Tom hopped on first, then Jake, and then Gaia was supposed to go. She just didn't make it the first time, so she kept running. Oliver hopped up easily.

Gaia could feel the train moving faster. She didn't want to be left behind here. She also didn't want to be the reason everyone else had to jump off. This was stupid. She had to get on. The big black open door of the freight car loomed over her, but she was just a little shorter than the two men and Jake, and she couldn't quite reach the metal handle.

"Gaia!"

She looked up to see an arm reaching for her. A dad-sized arm. She reached up for it and grabbed, and felt her feet leave the ground. As she twisted around, yanking her legs up so she could step on the small metal ladder-steps without getting herself chopped to bits, she suddenly realized she couldn't tell which man had grabbed her, Oliver or Tom. She looked up, still clinging tightly to the steps, ready to swing herself inside the door.

"Come on!" he yelled.

The only light was from the moon; they looked so alike. Was it Oliver? Was it Tom? Did it matter? There was a time when she hadn't even known which one was her father in the first place. So maybe it didn't matter. Maybe family was family, for better or for worse.

She reached out her free arm and grabbed him around the shoulders; his arm snaked around her and pulled her firmly into the train. She was safe. Whoever had done it, she was safe.

Amazing. Crazy and
amazing. Over the years, I've had
an interesting and varied relationship with the concept of "dad."
First my dad was the head of my
perfect little nuclear family—
though it was a little intense,
I'll admit. I was cut off from the
rest of the world and homeschooled,
and reading *The Canterbury Tales* in
Middle English at the age of ten,
not to mention being trained harder
than a circus performer in the
fighting arts. So first my dad was
my taskmaster and coach.

Then he was gone, and I was
furious. I had no dad at all for
what, five years? The whole time I
was dealing with my mom's death.

Then I thought Oliver was my
dad. And Oliver was evil, so I
had an evil dad.

Then I found my real dad, and
found out he was my real dad, and
saw the letters that told me he
had loved me all along. So I had
a dad again. A great dad. The dad
I'd always wanted.

Then my evil not-dad became my. . . well, my dependable uncle. And now my dependable uncle is acting like. . . a dad.

I don't know—I've spent my life feeling really unfortunate. I mean, I *have* been unfortunate. I've had a lot of horrible, horrible things happen to me and to the people I love. But maybe this is one way the universe is making it up to me.

Maybe that dad-face is finally going to be a face I can trust without asking myself who's behind it. Without wondering, "Is it my real dad? Is it the dad who's on my side?" Maybe anyone who looks at me with those eyes and that expression is someone I can count on. For once in my life, maybe I don't have to process that one bit of visual information.

All I know is, whoever grabbed me got me on this train. The arm that pulled me in was strong and safe. And I don't care which of those twins it belonged to. I trust them both. They both—sort of—feel like my dad.

Maybe there
was a
Hallmark card
she could
send. A soft-
focus picture **lost**
with fancy
script: *Just
Wondering If
You're Still
Evil?*

THE FREIGHT CAR WAS AS LONG AS

Quadrupled three taxicabs at least, and huge inside. Gaia was amazed. The only time she'd seen one of these had been in an electric train set, and it had been, well, about the size of her foot. It smelled musty, like too much stuff had been moved in and out of its ancient interior without a trip to the trainwash. It was an unidentifiable smell—sort of like grain, plus electronics, plus feet.

"Well, this is cheerful," she said.

She stood near the door, carefully holding on to the wall, feeling the slightly violent swaying of the train beneath her feet, and tried to figure out how to get comfortable. Finally, they all gingerly dropped to the wooden floor, which was somehow harder than concrete, and stared out the doorway at the rushing fields and woods they were passing.

"Well, the trip here was a lot more comfortable," Jake said. "What I wouldn't give for that pack of cards right now."

"Or the mystery sandwiches," Gaia laughed. "I'm freezing. I mean, literally. Should we yank that door closed?"

"At least partway," Tom said. He and Jake gave it a couple of tugs, and the ancient metal creaked its way close to shutting. Now the biting wind couldn't get to them, but the gloom was quadrupled. They huddled as near the dim moonlight of the doorway as they could.

Gaia and Tom were on one side of the door, Oliver and Jake on the other. There was nothing to do now but wait to get to Moscow. They rode, swaying with the train's movement, waiting.

"The trip up was much easier," Gaia said. "I feel bad."

"No need to apologize. This is the best way," Tom said. "They are going to be on the lookout for me. We can't be seen hopping into first class just a few miles from the prison I got out of. That'd just be asking for trouble."

"I guess. It was a nice ride, though. It's a shame they stuck you in a prison here—the mountains are gorgeous, and I saw some people who looked like they were on a horseback-riding trip or something. It looked like fun. But I'm sure you weren't noticing the lovely mountain peaks from your cell, huh?"

"Well, I've learned to find the good in whatever crazy situation I find myself in," Tom said. "Over the years, you know. You've had to do the same thing, haven't you? You found Washington Square Park even when you were living with George Niven and hating it."

"Well, it's a skill I could improve upon," Gaia admitted. "I mean, it's not something I work at. It's a lot easier to just be pissed off all the time."

"That, you've got a talent for," Tom teased.

Gaia laughed.

"Thank you," he added.

"For what?"

"For coming to get me. I'm quite sure that whatever Oliver did—and it's clear he did a lot—you were behind it. I know how you are. I wish you hadn't run such a risk, but I do appreciate it. And I'm glad to be out."

"Well, it was no problem." Gaia patted her father's leg. "Just another family adventure. I just wish I could have gotten here sooner. I felt so horrible, sitting around in the city while you were God-knew-where."

"I'll never know how you tracked me down. . . ." Tom shook his head. "This is no life for you to be leading," he said. "Too much danger, too much upheaval. You haven't had a moment to just be a normal girl, not in your entire life. When we get back, things are going to be different. We're going to settle down and be a family."

Gaia's chest began to tighten. She'd known that the subject of family and future would come up eventually. She just wished it didn't have to be now. But it *was* now. There was no more avoiding it. She'd have to tell her father the truth about Natasha and Tatiana. She'd just have to plunge right in and not let herself think about it.

"Dad," she started. Her voice cracked as she spoke. But her father didn't stop to let her speak. He seemed transported.

"You, me, and. . . I guess you know Natasha and I are going to get married. We'll really be a family. Just

163

pick up where we left off when I got poisoned and kidnapped. We'll finish that dinner, but this time I won't choke. That's a promise."

Gaia was silent.

"Gaia?"

Now, she commanded herself. *No more waiting. Just jump right in before he has another opportunity to interrupt.* She steeled herself, then took in a deep breath.

"Sssh!" Tom held a hand up.

Gaia stared into the darkness. She'd been so focused on the terrible truth at hand, she hadn't heard whatever was making him nervous. She was about to say something when—

"*Ugh!*" she shouted.

A pair of rough hands had reached out from the darkness and grabbed her around the throat. Clearly they weren't alone on the freight car.

GAIA ROLLED FARTHER INTO THE
pitch blackness with whoever had grabbed her. The stench was choking. Her attacker hadn't bathed in a long, long time, which meant he  probably wasn't well fed, either. If her eyes would just get used to the darkness, she could beat him, no

problem. But she had no way to gauge where he was, or whether he had friends.

"Gaia!"

"What happened?"

"There are squatters on the train—agh!"

From the sound of it, the others were being attacked, too. This was some way for their story to end—they'd made it out of a prison riot only to get jumped by some rail-riders for their pocket money? That wasn't going to happen. She stood, but the rocking of the train threw her down again. She felt hands scrabbling down her body, trying to find a wallet or money hidden in her pockets.

"Don't get fresh," she spat, using the distraction to jam an elbow into her attacker's face. She felt bone crunch against bone as his nose took the blow; maybe she'd broken it. That'd level the playing field a bit.

She crouched in the darkness, wishing she could get her back against a wall. "Where are you?" she yelled. "Dad! Open the door, someone open the door!"

She heard some "oofs" and "ughs" as Jake and Oliver and Tom fought their own individual battles, and then finally she heard the door roll wide open. The moon had risen while they were inside, and it spilled brilliant white light so bright it actually hurt Gaia's eyes. It was a good thing the night was clear. If she hadn't been able to see, she didn't know if she could have taken these attackers.

In the light, though, she could see what she was up against: not much. The vagrants were half-starved. The man who had attacked her looked young, but old before his time. He was missing every other tooth, and his hair was falling out—not from male-pattern baldness, but from malnutrition. It was obvious that he and his companions had spent too many cold nights eating too little food. And they were used to getting no resistance at all from the people they robbed.

Gaia's assailant jumped at her again. This time, she pulled her punches. A real blow from her could kill him. She wasn't ready to have blood on her hands. Not for this. She shoved him back and he grabbed her around the waist, trying to knock her to the ground once more. He was surprisingly quick. Plus, he was used to the swaying train and knew how to use it to his advantage. She tumbled back and hit the wall with her head. Momentarily dazed, she took a second to regroup.

"In the middle," Tom shouted. Their best bet, the four of them, was to somehow get back together and form a unified front at the center of the car. But the rail-riders were determined. Someone grabbed Gaia's hair, slammed her head against the wall one, two, three times. It made her angry more than it hurt.

"Cut it out," she growled. "*Ow.* What the—?" She grabbed her own hair and yanked it out of her assailant's grasp. She came face-to-face with a girl about her age, but filthy and visibly defeated by a difficult life.

Gaia was too angry to care. She decked the girl with a swift punch and kicked the other guy out of her way.

She got to the center of the car, where the other three were already together, and they stood back-to-back (-to-back-to-back, since there were four of them) to face the vagrant attackers. She thought there were about eight of them, but there might have been more. That explained why it smelled so bad in here. And now it was freezing, as the wind blew right in the wide-open doors. They all stood glaring at each other, the vagrants looking for any sign of weakness, Gaia and her crew just hoping they wouldn't have to do any more damage. Their packs had already been taken, dragged off to a corner to be plundered. The rail-riders had really hit the jackpot.

"Now, we're not going to need our camping supplies any longer," Tom said. "But I hope our travel documents are somewhere handy?"

"In a belt under my clothes," Oliver said. "Only... oh."

"What?"

"Well, the one that attacked me, he ripped it off. I can see it over there. That one has it. See?"

Gaia wanted to roar with frustration. A pint-sized man with enormous ears and spindly fingers had the belt in question. "That guy?" she asked. "I mean, we can take him. If someone gets my back, I'll go get it."

"Hang on," Tom said. He spoke in Russian, asking for the belt, and promising the rail-riders to give up everything else if they could just have their passports.

The guy answered with a laugh. He had a point. Why give up anything?

"We're going to have to go for it," Gaia said. "Come on, just cover me and I'll get it."

Without warning, Oliver leapt from his post and wrestled the belt-stealer to the floor, easily and handily, taking the belt without much of a struggle. The other vagrants started to attack, but he shoved them back with a vicious windmill kick that sent two of them flying—one nearly out the door.

"Oliver!" Gaia yelled. "That wasn't in the plan."

"Sorry. Too much discussion," Oliver said.

"But you didn't have to—"

"I had to get this back."

He had a point. Then again, his attack had been more vicious than Gaia thought necessary. But it broke their attackers. Any aggression the little hangdog band of enemies had had left was now spent. They settled down, almost literally licking their wounds and going through their newly acquired backpacks, pleased with all the camping equipment and, of course, the food.

"Should we try to get the rest of the stuff back?" Jake asked.

"We really don't need it," Tom said. "We probably would have dumped it all before getting on the plane. Easier if we travel light."

"He's right. May as well let them keep it," Oliver added.

Without another word, Gaia, Jake, Tom, and Oliver sank to the floor, making a little star, with their legs as the points sticking out. They were going to have to spend the rest of their trip vigilantly watching and making sure they kept the rail-riders at bay so they could keep the belt Oliver had fought so viciously for. There was no time for a heart-to-heart. Giving Tom the bad news about Natasha—that would have to wait.

Gaia sat, feeling an uneasy wave of confusion rising inside her. Oliver was good. She trusted him. He'd helped her all this way. But at the same time, that last confrontation—it had made her nervous. Fed into the suspicion her father had reawakened in her. If it had been Jake who'd taken the belt back with such fury, she would have chalked it up to being overenthusiastic and young. If it had been Tom, she'd have excused him because he was freaked out and tired and obviously having some kind of difficulty readjusting.

But it had been Oliver. And even with all the new-found trust he'd earned, Gaia found her mind returning immediately to Loki.

Who'd gotten that belt back? Oliver—or Loki?

Gaia needed to know. But it wasn't exactly the kind of thing you could just blurt out as a question. Maybe there was a Hallmark card she could send. A soft-focus picture with fancy script: *Just Wondering If You're Still Evil?*

Guess not.

Anyway, all she could do now was sit tight and hope to get to Moscow in one piece, with the other three in tow. She could figure the rest out later. For now, everybody in her little circle seemed trustworthy enough.

For now.

HOURS LATER, GAIA NOTICED THE

little sliver of scenery she could see through the slats of the door changing rapidly.

"We're getting close to Moscow," she said.

"What's the plan now?" Jake asked. "The train's slowing."

Faux Goatee

"We'll ride it into the station," Oliver said. "From there I can get us to the Metro, which we can take to the airport."

"What, like the subway?"

"Yes."

"Is that wise?" Tom asked. "I'd think the police would empty these freight trains before the homeless got to the city."

"Not in Moscow," Oliver told him. "The homeless problem is so big here, the homeless live in the train stations. There aren't any shelters. And if any police hassle us, we can bribe them easily."

"How do you know all this?" Gaia asked.

"Better that you don't know," he told her, and she heard that uncomfortable chord sound in her heart again. As Oliver, her uncle was mighty helpful; as Loki, he couldn't begin to make up for his horrible acts. After her initial rush of joy over having such a great ally, she was beginning to mistrust him again. . . or maybe her dad's attitude was rubbing off on her. Either way, she felt sort of lost.

The pale light of dawn vanished as they entered a long tunnel. It was too late now, anyway. They were on their way to the Moscow train station. If Oliver was right, they'd have no problem.

In short order, Oliver turned out to be a hundred percent right. The inside of the train station was like an underground version of the ritzier, normal station above. The minute the train stopped, their companions—now loaded down with their new, stolen camping equipment—filed off politely, saying good-bye to one another like tourists leaving a hostel on a backpacking trip, and barely glancing back at Gaia and her miserable little huddle. She finally shifted her position, feeling a horrible stiffness in her joints after so many hours of tense watching and waiting.

"Well, no sense sitting around," she said, and

hopped off after them. Tom, Oliver, and Jake followed after her. "Where to now?" she asked Oliver.

"This way," he said. "There's an entrance to the Metro system that's supposed to be for employees only. Follow me."

Tom looked around warily as they walked through the station. Gaia wasn't sure if he wanted them to stick with Oliver or set out on their own. She took him by the arm. "How are you feeling?" she asked him. "Are you still groggy?"

"I wasn't groggy," he snapped. "Just a little. . . disoriented."

"Okay, sorry." Gaia said. "Are you feeling better now?"

"Yes, I am. I'm just not sure about this," he told her.

"I know. What do you want to do?"

He turned toward her and studied her face. "What do you think we should do?"

Gaia blinked, a bit surprised. "Well. . . ," she said. "Actually, I think we should stick with the plan. Things have gone fine so far. And I don't want to leave Jake with someone potentially dangerous. If something goes wrong, it's three on one—I think we'll be okay."

He kept looking at her. "You really do, don't you? You trust Oliver."

She shrugged. "I think it's safer than taking off on our own." She paused a moment. "And yes. I actually feel okay about him."

Tom vanished into his thoughts for a moment. "I

have to tell you something," he said. "I'm really not well."

"I know," she said.

"Yes. Of course you would." Tom squeezed her arm back. "I'm going to have to follow your lead on this."

"Oh."

Gaia didn't want to take the lead on this. The consequences were so enormous. Besides, since she'd reconnected with her dad, she'd grown used to having him around for the big questions. Or at least wishing he was around to make the big decisions. Now he was here, and he was telling *her* to make the call?

That was a twist. Like being on a train where the conductor asks the passenger what stop is next.

But if that was the way it was going to be, she'd have to go with it.

"Okay," she said. "Then we stick to the plan." She tried to feel as confident as she sounded.

"I'm going to be watching carefully," he added. "I'm going to be watching Oliver for any signs of Loki. If he pulls anything suspicious—"

"It's okay." Gaia rubbed his bicep reassuringly. "I think it's going to be okay. It's one stupid plane ride— how much could go wrong?"

The minutes she said it, she wished she'd kept her mouth shut. He shot her a smile. "Let's just get back home and sort it out then," he said.

"Jake's got good news," Oliver said, slowing down

to join them. "He saved the pack that had the disguises in it."

"Jake!" Gaia cheered. "Look at you! How did you hide that?"

"I think they just didn't see it in all the confusion," Jake told her. "It was much smaller than the other packs and it was stuck behind me when we were sitting with our backs to each other."

"That's pretty impressive, Jake," Gaia said. Jake waved her off—he already knew how impressive he was.

They stepped into a utility room to pull their new act together. Oliver stuck an elaborate blond beard on his face—not too shaggy, but thick enough to cover the line of his jaw and make him look totally different. With his hair under a wig, he was unrecognizable.

Tom, on the other hand, went midlife-crisis groovy: he slicked his hair back with gel and lengthened it with a fake ponytail. Jake swapped a couple of items of clothing with him—a trendier sweater, too-young jeans.

"Wow, you look kind of slimy," Gaia commented.

"Well, thank you," Tom grumbled. "I'm so glad I had a daughter."

Gaia laughed. "Well, it's better than looking like an escaped prisoner. Maybe I should travel with you, and you can pretend I'm your girlfriend."

"That's much too disturbing," Oliver said, shaking

his head. "Gaia and Jake are going to be boyfriend-girlfriend, college kids traveling abroad. Tom and I will be on our own. We're going to travel in separate Metro cars from this point forward."

Gaia stopped laughing and turned to Oliver. She wanted to make sure she got the plan straight. And his expression was grave.

"Tom knows what I'm about to say. From now on, we do not know each other. This is the most dangerous leg of our trip. We're the most vulnerable here. We still do not know exactly who took Tom, but if the government is involved, they're going to have agents looking for us at the airport."

"They can't hold us. We can cause an international incident," Jake said.

"They can't arrest us legally, but they can 'disappear' us—we can be kidnapped easily. Try to stay in sight of official police whenever possible. Everybody have bribe money ready. And if you see someone else captured, keep going. An airport isn't the place for any kind of vigilante justice. Security is too tight. And if we all get taken, nobody knows where we are. The only chance we'll have is if one of us gets out and contacts someone to help us."

"And who the hell would that be?" Gaia demanded to know. "I needed you to get here in the first place."

"Don't worry. Your father has even better contacts than I do," Oliver pointed out. "But if worst comes to worst, I left information in my apartment. Whoever makes it back to the States can start the process over again. Or not," he said, with a glance at Tom. "That would be your choice."

He handed out their documents, rubles, and tickets. "Well, it's been nice knowing you," he said. "The Metro is down this corridor and to the right. You're taking the yellow line to the airport. Can't miss it." The door flopped shut behind him, and Oliver was gone.

Tom turned to Gaia. "Okay, I'm sticking to the plan," he said dubiously. "I hope you're right about this."

Gaia hugged him, careful not to dislodge his `faux goatee`. "I'll see you on the airplane," she said. "Just be careful."

She and Jake held hands—almost like a real couple, Gaia thought. As they left the closet and boarded the train, she saw their reflections in a window. It was amazing: After the night on the gross train, the days camping, they looked just like a shaggy hippie couple. It surprised her a little to see herself looking so normal. What surprised her more was how much she liked it. Not just looking normal, but looking normal holding hands with Jake.

She pulled her hand back. Not rudely. Just kind of slipped it out of his and pretended to be looking for something in her pocket.

"What are you looking for?" Jake asked. "Everything okay?"

"Yep, fine," she said, patting her leg like she'd just found whatever it was. The conditioned response she'd been having against normalcy had passed. When Jake reached for her hand again, she couldn't think of an excuse in the world not to let him.

And it felt really good. To let him hold her hand.

He looked down at her, smiling, like they were both in on a secret plan. Which, of course, they were. Except Gaia had the sudden realization that there was more between them than a shared mission and a Siberian adventure. She tugged his hand and looked up at him.

"I don't want you getting any ideas," she said.

"Ideas?" he asked.

"About us. When we get back to New York, we're still just friends. Really good friends. But that's all."

Jake looked at her, then shrugged nonchalantly. "Yeah, okay."

He kept her hand in his and gazed out the window of the train. Gaia tried not to feel disappointed that he wasn't arguing his case.

"You're okay with that?" she asked.

"Sure," Jake said. "Just friends. That's okay."

Once they arrived at the airport, Gaia and Jake stepped off. She looked up and down the long platform; sure enough, Oliver had been in the first car, her father in the third. She tried to pace herself so she'd always remain about thirty feet behind them—not so

177

close that they looked like they were traveling together, but not so far that she couldn't keep a close eye on everyone in her group.

The act of entering the airport and looking for their gate was easy. All they had to do now was get through the metal detectors and walk onto the plane. The airport was mobbed with people, teeming with tourists and business travelers. There was no way someone was going to mess with them here. Besides, the guards were about a hundred times more serious here than in JFK Airport in New York. For one thing, they carried Uzi machine guns. For another thing, they looked like they knew how to use them.

Gaia almost started to relax when Oliver made it through the metal detector and headed up the ramp toward their gate. She could see Tom's black ponytail as he waited his turn to go through the metal detector. Near him were two local police officers who looked no more official—or trustworthy—than the one who'd tailed her on the L train. They walked over to Tom, asking a few questions.

"I'm sure it's all right," Jake murmured, returning the squeeze she didn't know she was giving his hand.

It wasn't. It didn't seem to be. Now they pulled him out of the line, off to the side. He was answering their questions calmly, giving a perfect imitation of an annoyed but cooperative dude on the move. But they were eyeing him in a way that made Gaia uneasy. She started to move toward him. Jake jerked her hand back.

"We're on orders not to stop," he said.

"But Oliver's through," she said.

"Gaia. Orders. Stop it," Jake pleaded.

Gaia took her eyes off her father to make sure Oliver was through. If she saw him board the plane, she would go after her dad. Jake could go back with Oliver, and at least she'd be here to keep him company—with the kidnappers. Or in jail, or whatever. She wasn't going to leave him—

That was strange.

"What the—?"

Oliver had stopped to look back. He seemed to glance through the metal detectors, as though he were checking on them. She saw his eyes pass over her, then stop on her dad. Oliver's demeanor seemed to change a bit. He stiffened. What was he thinking? He was supposed to keep moving. His own orders.

She watched as he moved backward slowly, smoothly, almost like he was on roller skates. Without even turning around, he stepped inside a doorway and disappeared.

It was not the gate to the plane. Oliver was off course. She had no idea where he was, what he was doing, or what was happening.

He's deserting us, she thought. The thought

struck her with the full force of agony and betrayal. *My God. My dad was right. He turned us in, and now he's going to get his payoff. And I'm going to be captured next.*

She looked up at Jake. He'd seen Oliver disappear and looked puzzled. He turned his eyes to her.

How do I tell him? she thought. *We're dead. Oliver's gone. We're about to get snagged, and there's not a goddamned thing we can do.*

It was amazing
to watch how the
mirror-image
men, Tom in his
goatee and
Oliver **shatter**
in his regular
face, dusted
themselves off
in exactly the
same way.

GAIA WATCHED IN HORROR AS TOM

desperately but quietly tried to talk his way out of being detained. She couldn't stare at him openly—she was still hoping not to be recognized herself—so she was stuck in a frustrating and spastic dance of stealing quick glances and then looking away as if she didn't care.

Uzi Attention

But even the other passengers were beginning to notice what was going on. None of them liked the attitude of the pseudocops/kidnappers—Gaia knew that was what they were—hassling Tom. Before any real officers had a chance to notice them, the kidnappers took Tom by the arm and started to lead him away from the metal detectors.

Gaia stepped forward to interfere. All bets were off. If Oliver wasn't going to stick to the plan, then she wasn't going to either.

"Look," Jake said.

Oliver was stepping back out of the door. But he had taken off his disguise. Gaia breathed in sharply.

"Is he an idiot?" she asked.

Oliver patted his pockets as if he were just a regular Joe Tourist who thought he'd forgotten something. He stepped over to the metal detector and spoke to a

security guard. The guard nodded, and waved Oliver. . .
back through to the main terminal.

"Oh my God, where's he going?" Gaia breathed.

"He's going to get caught for sure," Jake said.

"I think. . . oh my God, I think that might be the point."

Oliver—Oliver, with his twin-of-Tom face—stood at the other end of the bank of metal detectors, looking around like a lost tourist. Showing his face to anyone who might be curious about him. Or looking for him. Or looking for someone who resembled him. Sure enough, almost immediately, he was approached by two more fake cops.

Gaia looked back over at Tom. His kidnappers had stopped short as their walkie-talkie squawked. The ones on the other side—the ones with Oliver—spoke intensely into their walkie-talkies. Each group was convinced he had Tom Moore, the escaped prisoner from Siberia. And each was telling someone—some central operative, giving them orders—that they had him.

If it hadn't been so nerve-racking, it would have been funny, Gaia had to admit. First Tom's captors tried to walk him out the door. Then they were ordered to stop, and the other captors headed for the opposite door. Neither group could see the other—by conicidence, Gaia and Jake were situated perfectly between them. But both groups were starting to attract attention. And neither wanted to give up their prize or lose credit for bringing in the quarry.

Gaia could guess exactly what was happening. Each group was trying to take credit for capturing Tom Moore. And each side was saying, "Those other guys don't have him. They have the wrong guy. *We* have the real Tom Moore." And as far as they knew, they were right. But the guy in the middle had to be getting frustrated.

Gaia just hoped he'd get really frustrated.

It was absolutely brilliant, what Oliver had done. By seeming to be Tom Moore, he'd created a perfect decoy. He had successfully confused the operatives so much, they were tripping over their own feet and messing up their own plan.

Of course, if it backfired, he'd be in that Siberian prison instead of Tom. Gaia watched anxiously, dividing her gaze spasmatically between her father and her uncle. The bad guys were waiting too long. They were arguing too much. They were attracting attention to themselves. Airport security attention. Uzi attention. . .

With a rush of relief, she saw similar packs of legitimate lawmen approach the two packs of would-be Tom-takers. Asking why they were bothering these tourists. Sending them on their way.

"Oh my God," Jake said. "They did it."

"*He* did it," Gaia added. "Oliver did. He distracted them long enough to get the real cops involved. He saved my dad."

184

"Again," Jake said.

Gaia nodded. She was painfully aware of that, and felt horrible for having thought there was even a dollop of Loki still in Oliver.

It was amazing to watch how the mirror-image men, Tom in his goatee and Oliver in his regular face, dusted themselves off in exactly the same way. Each one thanked the guard graciously, turned, and strolled unhurriedly through his metal detector. On the other side, they were both funneled into the same corridor, where they stood almost face-to-face, paused, and then walked, pretending not to know each other, to the gate.

By that time, Gaia was at her metal detector, too. She stepped through, then waited for Jake to follow her. She was surprised to find herself trembling from the tension of the moment. She had never seen such an elegantly choreographed yet accidental operation in all her life. It was high drama of the quietest kind. She swallowed hard and stepped through the gate onto her airplane. It was all she could do not to stop and jump for joy.

They were nearly there.

GAIA WAS WORRIED ABOUT THE plane ride back. She was

Suspicions

going to have to tell her

father about Natasha, and that was going to shatter him. She wasn't sure if he was back in control of his faculties quite yet. She didn't want to risk a confrontation between him and Oliver. Regardless of the way he'd helped them, Tom would no doubt hold Oliver responsible for Natasha's betrayal.

As a precaution, Gaia made sure her father sat at the extreme left side of the plane, and that Oliver sat on the extreme right. She even put both men in window seats. She was going to straighten this out, once and for all, and she didn't want her father distracted by Oliver's presence. The last thing she needed was an argument on her hands. On a twelve-hour flight, no less.

Once she had Tom settled, she walked across to Oliver. He and Jake had found a travel version of chess and were setting up the pieces, arguing quietly over who would get to be black.

"Oliver," she said. "I saw what you did."

He didn't look up. "Are you going to yell at me for going against my own orders?" he asked.

She laughed softly. "No. It was amazing."

He lined up the black pawns on his side of the board. "It was the least I could do," he said.

"If you'd been caught—"

"I would have dealt with the consequences." Oliver looked up. "I appreciate what you're saying, but it's not necessary. I just did what needed to be done. And it worked."

Gaia shook her head in admiration. Oliver was proving himself again and again and again. She could see that Jake totally admired him, too. Of course, he didn't understand the extent of what Oliver had done as Loki. But it was obvious how hard he was trying now.

"You'll be okay over here?" she asked Jake.

"Yeah, of course," he said. "Go sit with your dad. We'll be back in New York in no time."

Her father. Who she was going to be sitting next to for the next twelve hours or so, with no excuse not to give him the worst news he could ever hear.

"Hey," she said, flopping into her own seat next to him. "Now we can relax, right?"

"I suppose." Tom's gaze slipped across the plane, toward Oliver. He was nervous. He knew what Oliver had risked to get him on this plane—but he was a good agent, and he wasn't letting go of his suspicions. Gaia decided to let it go. No reason to force the issue. If Oliver really were reformed, her dad would figure it out in his own time.

"I'm glad you gave him this much of a chance," she said. "And so far, so good, right?"

"Yes," Tom said. "Yes, you were right about sticking to the plan. I'm just—"

"I know. He did a lot of terrible things. It's really, really hard to trust a man who tried to murder his own brother. But the brain's chemistry operates in mysterious ways. You're probably wise to be cautious at this point. I just have to say that so far, he seems nothing but sincere to me."

"Keep in mind that he's a true chameleon when he needs to be," Tom said. "It wasn't so long ago that he was still wreaking havoc. Let's not forget, he wouldn't have had to rescue me if he hadn't sent me to Siberia in the first place."

"Well, we don't know that he did that for sure," Gaia said. "Let's not forget, he was in a coma the night you choked. That's what we were celebrating, if you recall."

"Yes, well, I'm not entirely convinced that that's what happened." Tom said.

"Well, you gotta feel for the guy," Gaia said, pushing her seat into recline mode. "I've been working really closely with him. It's not that he doesn't remember his old life. He remembers everything, and he has to deal with all the terrible things he's done. A normal person might kill himself if he woke up to find he'd destroyed the lives of everyone close to him. But instead of running away, Oliver's trying to make amends. It doesn't fix things, but it counts for something, don't you think?"

Tom's answer was a long, light snore. Gaia had to laugh. Well, of course. He hadn't slept in days. He had just survived a brutal prison experience. They were all exhausted.

She adjusted his fake goatee, sticking the moustache part more firmly onto his face. She was just so glad to have him back. If only she didn't have one last, horrible task to perform.

She had to break his heart.

Nothing is ever what you expect it to be.

On the flight over here, I thought I'd be a wreck. I wasn't sure if my dad was even alive. I was anxious and nervous, yet I was enjoying myself. What was it? Anticipation? Hope? Looking forward to a big adventure? I remember talking to Oliver and being amazed at everything he said. Amazed that we were connecting on such a deep level. I was happy, I guess. Even with all the tension and worry, I was happy.

Now everything is okay. Dad is alive, and I've gotten him out of Siberia. We're heading home. When I dreamed of this trip, I imagined it would feel like a twelve-hour-long sigh of relief. Instead, it feels like slow suffocation. As devastated and betrayed as I felt when I found out about Natasha and Tatiana, Dad's going to feel worse. Much worse. Because he loved Natasha. And he left me with her. When he finds out she was a double agent, he's not just going to be heartbroken: He's going to feel guilty. And there's nothing I can do to stop him from feeling that way. I have my dad back, and I feel terrible.

How is that possible? *This* is supposed to be the happy trip. *That* one was supposed to be the tense trip. It's like the whole world has flip-flopped. For all I know, we're flying upside-down through Opposite World.

But there it is: The arms he thinks he's coming home to have been taken away in handcuffs. I've got to tell him, and I really don't want to.

God, I am such a coward. Maybe I can't feel fear, but engaging in emotional confrontation is my idea of terror.

I hope he sleeps the whole way back.

I know Gaia's father has been in a prison and that he's been drugged. And Gaia told me a little bit about how her uncle Oliver used to be a total asshole. I mean, I didn't get all the details, but she definitely hinted at some very dark stuff. Still, it seems like her dad could be a little more grateful.

I've never seen anything like this trip. Everything was orchestrated perfectly, and even when things went wrong, Oliver figured out a solution with lightning speed. I don't see how anyone could doubt the guy's sincerity.

Don't get me wrong: I'm sure there's a good reason for all the bad blood. But from where I'm sitting, it seems like someone as smart and sharp as Gaia's dad could read this guy and see something good in him. I mean, Gaia herself isn't exactly the trusting type. How long did I have to wait around before I could even get her to talk to me? Yet she

managed to find some common
ground with Oliver. Enough to get
herself here.

Not that it's any of my business. But when I peek across at
the other side of the plane, I
see Gaia watching her dad sleep,
and there's so much love in the
way she looks at him. More than
that. Much as I think she'd hate
to admit it, I think Gaia idol-
izes her dad. And I just hope the
guy deserves it. I hope he knows
something I don't, and that the
hostile feelings he has toward
Oliver are based in reality.

Oliver's an amazing man. I
could see myself learning a lot
from him. If he's done something
beyond forgiveness, I don't want
to know. There's too much to
learn.

TOM BLINKED AND OPENED HIS
eyes. Looking down, he could see New York off in the distance. He had slept for ten straight hours. He looked to his right. Gaia was awake, and she was smiling at him.

"I was out," he said.

"How do you feel?"

He thought about it for a moment. "Much more like myself," he said. "Much better." She handed him a small bottle of water and he drained it. Its refreshing coolness gave him an extra charge. He sat up and stretched.

"I was having the most fantastic dream," he said. "We were already home, and redoing that last dinner before I got kidnapped. Only this time it wasn't interrupted. I can't wait to get home."

"Uh, Dad. . ." Gaia's face fell.

"What's wrong?"

"I have to tell you something."

Tom was silent. He could tell it was bad news. Something Gaia was afraid to tell him, that was plain enough.

"Something happened to Natasha," he said. "Someone did something to her."

"Not exactly," Gaia said. "God, this is hard. I don't know how to start. . . . I started feeling suspicious when someone shot at me one night in a Ukrainian church. I was supposed to be meeting someone there."

194

"Shot at you!" Tom gripped Gaia's arm.

"I'm fine," she soothed him. "I got out of there. But after that, I tried to figure out who had set me up. Eventually, all the clues seemed to point closer to home than I would have liked."

"You're not saying—"

"I searched the apartment. Natasha and Tatiana's apartment. And I found a gun. The same gun that someone shot at me."

"It was planted. It was a plant."

"No. I hoped so, too. But then Dmitri helped me set up a sting. I let them think I'd be alone at a vacant lot in Brooklyn, and they showed up. . . and tried to. . ." Gaia's voice trailed off.

"You can't be serious."

"They tried to kill me, dad. Tatiana almost got away. And Natasha. . ." She couldn't look at him. "Natasha said horrible things. About us. About you."

"Natasha?"

Gaia stole a peek at her dad's face, then immediately wished she hadn't.

"I'm sorry. It's true. The CIA came and took them to jail. I had to make a deal with Tatiana to find out where you were—now that I found you, I have to call to let them know they can be jailed together. But they both admitted it. Proudly. They weren't who we thought they were."

Tom's face folded into a tight, closed-up package.

"But we're still a family," she said.

He didn't move.

"You and me. We have each other. Not that that's the same. But it's something."

His eyes closed. He nodded slowly. "Of course," he said. "Yes. We have each other."

But Gaia had blown out a candle, and Tom's soul was dark as a result. Any idiot could see that.

Poof.

And it was
Gaia's
words, the
ribbon of
air **piercing**
coming out
of her
mouth, that
had done
this to him.

THERE ARE CERTAIN THINGS A KID

should never have to do—even a kid who's been on her own since she was twelve. And breaking her father's heart is one of them. Gaia stood outside herself and watched, her gut melting with the pain of it, as her father stared

straight ahead. Behind his impassive face, she knew he was flicking through his Rolodex of memories, reliving every moment with Natasha, then smacking himself with the reality that each kiss, each kind word, each loving gesture had been a cold, empty lie. Trying to wrap his mind around the staggering loss. And it was Gaia's words, the ribbon of air coming out of her mouth, that had done this to him, choked off the only good thing in his life. Dug up the seedling of the future that he'd nurtured.

Their little hopes for a normal family had been blown apart in one tiny conversation, whispered from the aisle seat to the window seat.

The worst part was that no matter how hard she tried, Gaia couldn't soften the blow. She was so goddamned clumsy with her words, she felt like she had made it worse. When she fought, everything made sense, she could measure her strength to that of her opponent. But this? Words? Feelings? She couldn't control how hard they hit or how they made someone feel. She'd had chance after chance on this long trip, and she had put it off so long that the information had just come out in a `diarrhealike rush.` Gaia hated herself.

"Dad?" she asked, lamely. "Are you okay?"

"I'm fine," he said. He looked down, avoiding her face, as he unbuckled his seat belt. Gaia realized that the plane had landed and taxied all the way to the gate in the time she'd been in agony over this. She hadn't even noticed. She unbuckled herself and stood up. They started the long, slow shuffle to the front of the plane. In the other aisle, Oliver and Jake were making the same journey, the two men yards apart in space and miles apart in emotions. Gaia realized her father would never forgive Oliver now. He would be sure it was Oliver who'd turned Natasha against him. It was one more nail in the already-sealed coffin of their relationship.

She locked eyes with Jake and tilted her head toward the exit. He made a confused face. She eyeballed the exit again, trying to indicate to him that he should take Oliver and get him into a separate cab. She didn't know how upset her dad would be. She didn't want a confrontation in the airport. But it was no use. She just looked like `a head-bobbing, eye-rolling idiot.` Jake just shrugged, and Gaia stopped to tie her shoe so they would at least be forced to leave the plane first.

Out in the airport, Oliver and Jake waited for them. Tom walked slowly, his head bent toward the floor. Gaia approached them.

"I was thinking, we'd probably better split up. There isn't enough room at the Seventy-second Street apartment for all of us; you can stay with Oliver in Brooklyn till he decides it's safe for you to go home. Does that make sense?"

Her words hung in the air. Jake and Oliver looked curiously at Tom, who gave them the super–poker face. He stood there like a pillar of concrete.

"We'll see you soon?" Oliver asked. He directed his question toward Gaia, ostensibly, though he was looking at his brother.

"Sure. Sure, we will. After everyone gets settled in and rested," Gaia said, taking her father's arm.

Oliver, sensing that this would be the wrong time to force a brotherly moment, turned away, heading for the doors to the taxi stand. Jake hesitated and looked at Gaia.

She looked back.

"I'll call you?" he asked.

"Definitely," she said quickly.

"Not because I'm getting ideas," he said.

"Of course not. Just to hang out."

"Right." He nodded.

The block of concrete to her left was no help. Gaia felt as awkward and exposed as a fresh septum-piercing. The truth was, she was the one with ideas. About Jake. Serious ideas. And that was the last thing she needed: more romantic entanglements. Ed, she missed terribly. He just knew how to make her laugh like no one else. And she loved him for that. And Sam. . . She wasn't sure how she felt about Sam, but it pretty much wavered between guilt and lingering love. But after this intense little adventure, she thought Jake was maybe the only guy who had ever understood her—who would ever understand her.

Yikes. She wondered whether that was good or bad. If you know there's nobody out there who can understand you, you've always got a buffer zone, something they can't penetrate. But if you think someone actually *does* get your inner workings. . . you set yourself up for danger.

Being alone seemed like the obvious solution.

Except that when she was alone, she was miserable.

I've never wanted to hug someone so much in my whole life. The last few days have been so intense. I swear, Gaia and I lived a lifetime together. She told me so much about herself—more than she's ever told anyone, I'm sure of that. That's a huge deal. And a huge responsibility. I just wish there was some way I could tell her I understand that, and that I'm not going to let her down.

Who am I kidding? The most surefire way to make Gaia run screaming for the hills is to say that to her directly. It's probably a blessing in disguise that her dad and uncle had to split up before I could try to get my arms around Gaia—or kiss her. I need to take some time to chill out so I don't scare her off. Ease back into my regular life.

My regular life. Wow. That sounds so far away. I guess a lot of people would feel as if they couldn't wait to get back to some

old familiar ground, but I just
want to tell this cab to turn
around and go back to the airport
so I can get on another plane.
I've heard that war reporters get
addicted to adrenaline and can't
function if they're not trying to
type on their laptops while
they're dodging bullets. I think
I understand them. I'm never
going to be regular again. I'll
do what I have to do—bide my
time, keep my grades up, train
until my body's a perfect weapon—
but I'm going to do this again.
And again and again. Maybe I'll
join the CIA, or some other spy
organization I don't even know
about. I'll have to do my
research. But I'm never going to
be Regular Guy.

Never have been, and now I
know I never will be.

GAIA OPENED THE DOOR TO THE

East Seventy-second Street apartment slowly. Empty apartments have a smell to them, of dry heat mixed with dust. She wished they didn't have to come back here. To the house of hope. To the bed where Tom and Natasha used to sleep. But there was nowhere else to go.

Another Univers

At least her dad seemed calmer. The taxi ride had been good for him, apparently. At least he wasn't talking to himself anymore.

"You can have the first shower," she said, giving him a smile. "I'll order up some food, how about that? Pizza? Or something more nutritious? Um. . . burritos?"

"Whatever you like," he said, with a tired smile that was supposed to be reassuring but just looked. . . tired. "Something that will go down easy. My stomach—"

"Yeah. Like soup or something. I'll figure it out."

"Okay."

"There's ointment and stuff in there. Oh! Wait a second." She darted into the master bathroom and swept all of Natasha's feminine belongings—her cosmetics, her shampoos—into a bucket and shoved it all under the sink. She'd change the sheets on the bed while he was showering. She was going to make this as easy as possible for him. She'd do anything to have him back.

She stepped out of the bathroom, letting him go

in, and closed the door behind him. *Phew.* First things first: Gaia had to call Dmitri and tell him to give the go-ahead to send Tatiana to her mother's jail cell. She didn't want to give them that. But she had made a promise. She picked up her cell phone, sitting in its charger on the floor next to her bed, and hit the speed-dial. The old Russian man answered on the first ring.

"I'm back," she said. "He's here. Everything's fine."

"That's good," Dmitri said. "Are you all right?"

She sighed. "Sure. But telling him about Natasha was horrible. I felt so bad."

"It can't be helped."

"I suppose. But you can tell them Tatiana can have her little reward."

"I'll do that." Gaia heard the line click off and looked at the screen, ready to dial the diner downstairs, when she noticed the little envelope at the top of her screen.

A message.

She listened and was shocked to hear Sam Moon's voice. It sounded like he was a million miles away, like a voice from another universe. Another lifetime. But when Gaia thought about it, she realized that she had just seen him the other day. On Broadway, when she'd come out of Urban Outfitters. He had moved to an apartment. He was restarting his life without her. Now he was calling her.

"I wanted to tell you where I'm working," he said

in the first message. "I mean, not where I'm living, or anything. I still need more time. But, ah, free food and all. I know how you like that, so if you want to come by. . ." He left the address, and hung up.

And there was another one. "Hi. Uh, yeah, so you didn't come by and that's cool, but I wanted you to know you can. I know yesterday I said I still needed time, but I didn't mean that completely. I've been thinking a lot about it, and I think with a little distance I can understand a bit better why you were so guarded. Why you acted the way you did. I came on too strong, and that was, you know. That was my deal. So I won't do that again." He paused. "I think I'm ready," he added. "I'd really like to try again. I'd love to give it a try. So. Call me. When you feel like it."

What? What did this mean? Gaia felt a tightening in her chest. Two messages in a couple of days. From Sam. From Sam Moon. Sam Moon had called her. Sam Moon had called Gaia Moore to say he wanted to give their relationship another shot while she'd been in Siberia battling the unknown operatives who had kidnapped her father, with the help of her formerly evil—possibly not evil—uncle and a random guy who was now her best friend.

But not just her best friend. He was someone whose heart seemed to match hers, and it was all she could do to stop herself from thinking about him.

Life. Life was just bizarre sometimes.

Dear Dad: Sorry I had to break your heart. Sorry I can't fix anything. Most of all, I'm sorry I'm thinking about Sam and Jake when you need me the most.

I'm also *really* sorry we're not on that freight train, fighting with thieving vagrants, or building a shelter in the middle of the frozen steppe, or even running around in the middle of a prison riot. Because all those things were easier for me than figuring out this knotty little conundrum.

Sam was the love of my life. Is. Was. Is. Was.

Jake is the best thing that's ever happened to me. But I don't know what I should do about it.

Neither one of them should matter, because you're here, and you're hurting, and I have to be there for you—not flying off the handle every time a guy calls me.

So please excuse me if I'd rather fly off to somewhere even

farther than Siberia to kick some
ass—any ass. Any ass at all.
Because you know what? It's easier. Matters of the ass-kick are
easier than matters of the heart,
any day.

And you heard it here first.

here is a
sneak peek of
Fearless™ #30:
FREAK

The last
thing she
wanted right
now was to

trepidation

open a

can of

emotionally

overwrought

worms.

GAIA MOORE WAS HAVING A MOMENT

Damn Guardian Angel

she'd probably remember forever. She was one of those rare people who had burned-in-her-memory moments all the time, but this one was different from the norm.

This one was good.

A good memorable moment was atypical in Gaia's screwed-up life. The awful ones. . . well, those came up all the time.

Like the moment she learned her mother was dead. The moment she realized that the man she thought was her father might actually be her evil uncle, Loki. The moment Mary passed away. The moment Sam was kidnapped. The moment some Loki operative fired shots at Ed. The list of gut-wrenching, miserable, devastating moments went on and on.

But a light, content, all-is-right-with-the-world moment—that came almost never. And when she realized she was having one, instead of automatically thinking of the few things that were still wrong—things that could crap all over the moment like a giant pigeon—Gaia just smiled.

For once, she was going to let herself be happy.

"I like this," Jake Montone said, lying back next to Gaia on the big mound of rock near the Columbus

Circle entrance to Central Park. "Who would've thought there was actually a place in this city where you could see stars? Actual ones, I mean. Famous people I've been seeing everywhere lately. It's like you get one warm day and they suddenly come out of hiding. I was almost nailed by Brad Pitt on rollerblades this afternoon in Union Square."

"Jake?" Gaia said, the back of her skull searching for a smooth bit of rock to rest on.

"Yeah?" he asked. He turned his head so he was looking at her profile.

"Shut up," she said.

"Right."

Ever since Gaia, Jake, and Oliver had returned from their little smash-and-grab job in the former Soviet Union (they'd smashed a fortress and grabbed Gaia's dad, Tom), Jake had been prone to these little fits of verbosity. Just every once in a while. Like he was a little kid who was still psyched up from a trip to an amusement park and couldn't contain his bursts of excitement. Gaia would never have admitted it, but somewhere deep down she kind of thought it was cute—in an irritating sort of way.

A jagged point bit into the back of her head and she moved again, sighing in frustration. Jake sat up, slipped out of his denim jacket, bunched it into a ball and moved to prop it under the back of her head. For a split second Gaia thought about refusing, making a

4

crack about his chivalry and turning it into a joke, but she stopped herself. Instead she just lifted her head, then leaned back into the Jake-scented softness.

Ah. Pillow. Just one more thing to make the perfect moment last.

All is well, Gaia thought, taking a deep breath. She almost didn't dare to believe it, but it was true. Her father was home, safe and sound. Her uncle had been living for days now as good old normal Uncle Oliver, with no signs of Lokiness whatsoever. There was no one out there hunting her down, tracking her every move, plotting ways to take her out.

And to top it all off, she had a new friend. A real friend. Surprisingly enough, Jake Montone had turned out to be, contrary to all snap judgments, a non-moron. He was, in fact, freakishly true. Supportive. Noble almost.

"I can't believe that guy actually gets to have sex with Jennifer Aniston," he said suddenly, his brow furrowing beneath his dark hair.

Okay, so he was also still a guy. But he had already saved Gaia's life, accepted her increasingly psychotic family situation with none but the pertinent questions asked, *and* dropped everything to come to Russia with her to save her father. In a short time he'd gone beyond the call of duty, friendshipwise. He'd gone beyond the call of duty for a damn guardian angel.

"So, anybody at school ask where you were for the past few days?" Jake asked.

"Not really. The teachers are used to me disappearing, and no one else notices."

Except Sam, Gaia thought, her heart giving an extra-hard thump. *Sam noticed.* Sam had noticed to the tune of eight messages on her answering machine. Gaia had been more than a little surprised when she'd heard his voice over and over and over again on the tape. The last time she'd seen the guy he'd basically told her to get out of his life and stay out. By the time she was done listening to his messages it was fairly clear that he wanted the exact opposite.

I need to call him back, Gaia thought. But even as her brain formed the suggestion, the rest of her felt exhausted by the mere thought. The last thing she wanted right now was to open a can of emotionally overwrought worms. She'd much rather just stay where she was—lying on her back in the park, staring at the sky, with Jake's warmth next to her, keeping the goosebumps at bay.

"So, listen," Jake said, propping himself up on his elbow and turning on his side.

Gaia swallowed and her stomach turned. It was a loaded "so listen." The kind that was usually followed by either an unpleasant announcement like, "So listen, I'm moving to Canada." Or by an awkward silence–inducing question like, "So listen, do you want to go to the prom?" Not that Gaia had ever been asked to a prom before, but she could still identify the appropriate "so listen."

She stared at the sky and held her breath, waiting for the ax to fall, not sure which ax would be the quicker, less painful one. Gaia had been getting the more-than-a-friend vibe from Jake for a few days now, but she'd chosen to ignore it. Mostly because acknowledging it would require acknowledging the fact that she was also attracted to him, and Gaia was definitely not ready to go there.

Not just yet.

Whenever she allowed herself to admit she liked a guy, only anguish ensued.

"I was wondering if you might want to—"

Jake's question was interrupted by a sudden, blinding light that was directed right into his eyes. He held up his hand to shield himself, and the beam moved to Gaia's face. She squinted against the stinging pain and sat up, her boots scraping against the grainy surface of the rock.

"What do you kids think you're doing out here at this hour?" an authoritative voice asked.

The light finally moved away and Gaia was able to distinguish the outlines of two New York City policemen through the pink dots that were floating across her vision.

"Just hanging out," Jake said, pushing himself to

his feet. He was slightly taller and more than slightly broader than either of the men in blue.

"Yeah, well, not the safest place to just hang out these days," the chubbier of the two cops said, eyeing Gaia as she stood. He shone his light along the ground, looking for beer cans, crushed joints—anything that would allow him to give Jake and Gaia more than the usual amount of hassle.

"We've had a number of attacks in this area of the park in the past few days," Cop Number One said. "I suggest you two move it along for your own safety."

"Sure," Jake said, leaning down to grab up his jacket. "No problem."

He used his jacket to nudge Gaia's arm, and they turned and scrambled down the side of the boulder. Gaia sighed as she fought for her footing on the steep side of the rock. She appreciated what the cops were trying to do, but they'd obliterated her perfect moment. Of course, they might have also saved her from an awkward, embarrassing, tongue-tied conversation with Jake about his "so listen." Little did they know they'd just added "rescue from ill-fated romantic interludes" to their duties as New York's finest.

Gaia jumped the last few feet to the ground and landed next to Jake. He shoved his arms into his jacket and straightened the collar as they started to walk. For a few blissful seconds there was total silence—aside from the faint honking of car horns somewhere out on the streets that surrounded the park.

Then Jake tried again. "So, anyway, as I was saying—"

"Hey! No! Help! *Help!*"

It took Gaia a split second to realize that she wasn't hearing her own desperate get-me-out-of-here pleas, but actual shouts of panic.

"It's coming from over there," Jake said, taking off.

Gaia was right at his heels, slicing through the trees in the direction of what was sounding more and more like a struggle. They suddenly emerged into a small clearing and saw not one but two middle-aged women in jogging suits, flattened on their backs by four men in full-on black. Two of the men held each victim down, while the other two yanked at their clothes.

Gaia took one look at the tear-stained and desperate face of the woman closest to her and felt her fingers curl into fists.

"Hey!" Jake shouted at the top of his lungs.

All four men stopped and whipped their heads around. At the instant of surprise, Jake and Gaia both launched themselves at the clothing-gropers and knocked them off their victims. As Gaia tumbled head over heels with her man, she saw the two women struggle to their feet.

"Go!" Gaia told the joggers, as she flipped the assailant over and dug one knee into his back. A second guy wrapped his arm around her and yanked her off his friend.

The stunned, shaken women pulled themselves together, then wisely turned and ran. Gaia was thrown away from her second man and she had to fight for balance. The second she found her footing she got her game face on. Jake was working his best Matrix-worthy moves on his two guys as Gaia's men circled, leering at her.

"We got the girl, Slick," one of them said, punctuating his statement by spitting at her feet. "Aren't we lucky?"

Slick looked Gaia up and down slowly. "You said it, buddy."

If you're feeling so lucky, come and get me, Gaia thought. *Quit wasting my time.*

Slick came at her then with a clumsy one-two punch, which she easily blocked. She thrust the heel of her hand up into his nose, waited for the satisfying crack and the spurt of blood, then turned around, hoisted him onto her back and over her shoulder. He landed on the ground in front of her, clutching his nose, rolling back and forth, and groaning in pain.

Gaia looked up at his friend and lifted her eyebrows. "Ready?"

He let out a growl and ran at her. Gaia was about to throw a roundhouse at him when Jake shouted her name. She looked up at the last second and saw a third guy coming right at her from her left. Glancing at his trajectory, Gaia quickly ducked, crouching as low to the ground as possible. She smiled when she heard the *thwack*, then stood up and slapped her hands together.

Both of the thugs were laid out on the ground, unconscious. They'd smacked heads coming at her and knocked themselves out. It was almost too easy.

"Amateurs," Gaia said under her breath, stepping over one of the bodies.

"Nice work," Jake told her, reaching out his hand. They slapped palms and Gaia noticed that the fourth guy was also unconscious, crumpled into a seated position against a tree.

"You too," she said.

They both looked up when they heard rustling in the dark and the huffing and puffing of approaching men. The two cops who had roused them from the boulder came skidding into the clearing, hands on their holsters. They took one look around at the men on the ground, then gazed at Gaia and Jake, stunned.

"What happened here?" Chubby Cop asked, looking impressed against his will. "I thought we told you two to move along."

"And we did," Jake said, opening his arms. "You're welcome."

Cop Number Two shot Jake a wry smile as he knelt

11

down to cuff Slick. "And now you can hang out while we get your statements, wiseguy," he said.

Gaia and Jake exchanged a quick smile and leaned back against a thick tree trunk to wait, catty-corner from one another. The side of Gaia's shoulder pressed into the back of Jake's, and she didn't move away.

"They're gonna take credit for this, aren't they?" Jake whispered.

"Probably," Gaia replied.

"Figures. I feel like Batman. I keep kicking ass and there's no one I can tell about it," Jake said. Then he smiled and nudged his shoulder back into hers. "'Cept you."

Gaia felt the corners of her mouth tugging up slightly. What was wrong with her? Was she actually *enjoying* flirtation?

"So, Gray's Papaya after this?" Jake asked as the cops roused the two knuckleheads who had run into each other.

Gaia's stomach grumbled. "Definitely."

She tucked her chin and turned her face away from him, smiling for real. She'd been doing this forever—beating up toughs in the park, ducking or dealing with cops, then going for a postfight midnight snack. But she'd been doing it forever alone. And she'd always thought that was the way she liked it. Yes, actually—that was the way she *had* liked it.

But now . . . now she liked having someone there.

She liked having Jake to share all this with. She liked having an . . . ally.

Huh. Maybe it's true, Gaia thought, an evening breeze tickling a few strands of her long blonde hair against her face. *Maybe things can change.*

TOM MOORE SAT AT THE SMOOTH

 metal table glaring across at the prisoners. His spine was straight, his fingers clasped into a knot, his elbows just slightly off the edge of the table top. He breathed in and out deliberately, maintaining his composure—maintaining his calm.

Just another set of criminals. Just another day.

"Are you going to say anything?" Natasha asked.

"I'll ask the questions," Tom spat back instantly. He could taste the venom in his own mouth.

Just another set of criminals. Just another day.

Tatiana blinked but remained otherwise impassive. She looked small and wan, her light skin translucent and green in her bright orange jumpsuit. The monstrous cuffs circling her tiny wrists were almost comical. Even though it was impossibly cold in the interrogation room, there was a line of sweat visible above her upper lip. It was taking a lot more effort for Tatiana to

13

remain composed after days of stony, obstinate silence in her cell. Far more effort than her more experienced, more world-weary, more spy game–weary mother.

Tom shifted his gaze to Natasha again. Her dark hair was pulled back in a low braid that hung heavy and smooth down her back. She wore an amused smirk on her face. The face he had once held, once kissed, once touched with the tenderness that he'd formerly reserved only for his wife—his one true love.

His stomach was shot through with hot acid bitterness. He could only hope the nausea wasn't apparent on his face.

"That's fine," Natasha said finally, shifting slightly in her iron chair. "It's just that you're not. Asking questions, that is."

"Who were you working for?" Tom asked flatly.

The smirk deepened. "You don't want to know that, Tom."

"Don't say my name," he snapped. "You don't have that right."

Maddeningly, the smirk turned into a smile.

"Who were you working for?" he repeated.

"I want to talk about a deal," she said.

Tom got up and threw his chair across the room, the noise slicing his eardrums as it clattered and crashed. Tatiana flinched as he leaned his knuckles into the table and got right in Natasha's face.

"You tried to kill my daughter! You tried to *kill*

Gaia! And you have the audacity . . . the unmitigated *gall* to sit here and talk to me about a *deal*!?" he shouted, his eyes so wide they felt about to burst.

She didn't move. She didn't blink. And suddenly Tom Moore knew. He knew that he was going to grab her. He saw his hands around her throat. Saw himself choking the life out of her. Who would blame him if he did it? The woman deserved to die.

"Agent Moore!"

The door to the cinder block–walled room flew open and Director Vance stood on the threshold, his intimidating former-Navy-Seal, former-NCAA-basketball-player frame blocking out the light from the hallway. He pressed his full lips together into a thin line.

"That's enough, Agent Moore," Vance said in his rumbling baritone.

Tom didn't move. His knuckles turned white against the table as he continued to glare into Natasha's unwavering eyes.

I told this person I loved her. I thought I was going to be with her forever, he thought. The visions he'd had of him and Natasha together, of making a family with their daughters, flitted through his mind, whirling together in a sickening tornado of colors.

"Agent Moore, I'm not going to ask you again," Vance said, stepping into the room.

The whirling suddenly stopped. Tom swallowed

hard and struggled to focus on Vance. Ever so slowly, some semblance of balance returned to his mind and he realized what he was doing. He was letting Natasha get the upper hand. He was letting her have the whole game. He pushed himself up and smoothed down the front of his blue suit jacket, hoping to regain some shred of dignity.

But when he glanced at her again it was clear from the expression of triumph on her face that all was lost. He couldn't handle being around her. He'd just proven it.

Tom turned and followed his director out of the room and into the monitoring space just beyond. A couple of agents stood in front of the one-way mirror that looked over the interrogation room and they averted their eyes when Tom entered. The second the door was shut behind him, Vance turned on Tom, his dark eyes livid, his deep brown skin flushed with anger.

"Moore, don't you ever let me see you lose your cool like that with a prisoner again, you understand me?" Vance spat, leaning in over Tom. "You know what you were in that room? You were that prisoner's bitch!"

Tom pulled his head back slightly, unaccustomed to such severe scolding after his glorious tenure in the CIA. Still, he knew on some level that Vance was right, so there wasn't much he could say.

"I'm sorry, sir," he said, swallowing his pride. "It won't happen again."

"Damn right it won't. Because you're going home,"

Vance said through his teeth.

It took Tom more time than absolutely necessary to process this. The man couldn't be suggesting that he was taking Tom off this case. Didn't he know how invested in this he was? He had to find out who had kidnapped him, who had ordered his daughter to be killed. He had to find out for sure whether or not his brother, Oliver, was involved, as he so highly suspected.

"What?" Tom spat out finally. "No! Sir, I—"

"You heard me, Moore," Vance said, straightening his tie and shooting a death glare at the few CIA personnel who had conspicuously stepped into the room to watch the proceedings. "These particular prisoners obviously have you more than a little on edge." He paused for a breath and looked at Tom sorrowfully, almost pityingly. "You're taking a little time off," he added, causing Tom's heart to sink with the finality of it all. "Starting now."

GAIA OPENED THE DOOR TO THE

Manic

East Seventy-second Street apartment on Friday after school and immediately went on alert. She lifted her hand, telling Jake to stop and wait behind her, then pushed the door open the rest of the way as slowly and quietly as possible. Something was wrong—she could feel it.

There was a crash in Natasha's—no, her *father's*—bedroom. She and Jake glanced at each other. There was someone here.

Dammit, Gaia thought. *I knew it wouldn't last.*

She tiptoed toward the living room, her rubber-soled boots soundless on the hardwood floor. For once, Gaia was clueless as to who she might find. Could there be a *new* enemy? Was it even possible?

Footsteps approached, confident and loud and not remotely trying to be stealthy. Gaia flattened herself against the nearest wall, around the corner from the hallway, and braced for a fight. That was when her father emerged into the room, all smiles.

"Hey, honey!" he said, shuffling a few envelopes in his hands. His dress shirt was unbuttoned at the top and the sleeves were rolled up above his wrists. "I didn't hear you come in!"

Clearly, Gaia hadn't fully acclimated to civilian life. The idea of coming home to her *father* of all people was still so very strange.

Tom's eyes flicked to Jake, who was now standing outside the door to the kitchen, his muscles visibly slackening.

"Hey, Jake," Tom said as Gaia forced her fingers and her jaw to unclench.

Her father breezed by her and sat down at the head

of the dining-room table, where there were dozens of neatly arranged piles of bills and papers. He started pulling pages out of the envelopes, sorting them, and tossing the envelopes into the kitchen garbage can, which had been temporarily relocated.

Gaia finally moved away from the wall, eyeing her father. This was all very weird. Not only was he home in the middle of the day, but he was doing paperwork—something she hadn't seen him do . . . ever. When her mom had been alive, that had been her territory, and since then, her father hadn't been around for enough days in a row to even know that there *were* bills.

On top of it all, there was an odd air about him. He was humming. His foot was bouncing under the table. Her father was normally cool, aloof, sometimes intense, but always in a quiet way. Just then he was acting. . . well, hyper.

"Dad?" Gaia asked, tucking her hair behind her ears. "Everything okay?"

"Fine. Great, actually," he said, glancing up at her for a split second before returning his attention to the papers.

Jake moved into the room, stuffing his hands into the front pockets of his jeans and giving Tom wide berth. The two of them hadn't gotten along very well on the whole Russia excursion, and it was clear that Jake also sensed something off in Tom's behavior.

"I heard a crash in the bedroom," Gaia said, sitting down in a chair across from her father. She pulled her messenger bag off over her head and laid it carefully on the floor. Normally she would have just dropped it, but something told her not to make any sudden noises or movements. Her father, though acting happy, was clearly on edge.

"Right, I broke a lamp," her father said. "I'll clean it up later."

Gaia looked at Jake and he tilted his head, giving her a look that said, "He's *your* father."

"Okay, so what are you doing home?" Gaia asked, glancing at her black plastic watch. "It's four o'clock."

"I decided to take some time off," Tom said, slapping a piece of paper down on top of a pile. Gaia felt as if he'd just slapped *her*. Her father taking time off? Was this some kind of new, previously unexplored reality? Before she could even formulate a question, her father paused and folded his hands in front of him, flattening a stack of what looked like contracts. "In fact, there's something I wanted to talk to you about," he said with a smile. "How would you feel about making a new start?"

"What kind of new start?" Gaia asked slowly.

"Should I. . . ?" Jake asked, motioning toward the bedrooms.

"No, stay," Tom said with a laugh. "I just wanted to ask Gaia how she'd feel about doing a little shopping this weekend."

Gaia's jaw dropped, but she recovered quickly and

snapped it shut again. That was definitely a phrase she'd never thought she'd hear. Not from her father, anyway. The things she heard most often from him were phrases like, "Stay off the radar," "I'll try to be in touch some time next month," and "Aim for the solar plexus."

"Shopping?" Gaia asked, slumping back in her seat. "For what?"

Please don't let him say bras or something like that, Gaia thought. *Like he suddenly wants to make up for not being there and for my not having a mother.*

Gaia didn't blame her father for his many disappearing acts over the years—at least not anymore— not now that she knew what he'd been doing on all those excursions and why. He'd been fighting the good fight. Protecting her—protecting the free world. It had taken Gaia a long time to accept that and move on. She couldn't handle it if he decided to take on the role of guilt-ridden father now.

"New furniture," Tom said. "Everything in this place belongs to Natasha and Tatiana. I think it's time we get some of our own things, don't you?"

A little stirring of excitement came to life in Gaia's chest. She hadn't thought of it that way, but her father was right. This place was going to be their home. *Their home.* She and her father hadn't had one of those in years. Why would they want it to be decorated by their evil archenemy?

"Really?" Gaia said, too unaccustomed to the idea of doing something as normal as furniture shopping with her father.

"Yes, really," Tom said, standing. He moved over to the end of the hallway and looked off toward the opposite end—toward the room Gaia once shared with Tatiana. "We can get rid of those two beds and get you a double . . . move out that old fashioned desk—I'm guessing it's not your style," he added with a grin.

Gaia liked what he was saying, but the way he was saying it was still odd. Almost manic. He was too excited about the prospect of shopping.

But maybe he should be, Gaia thought. *Maybe he wants some normalcy in his life as much as I do.*

She sat up straight and squared her shoulders. "Okay, I'm in," she said.

"Good," her father said, squeezing both her shoulders from behind. "We'll go over to Seventh tomorrow and hit the stores." He turned, hands in the pockets of his khakis, and looked around the living room. "It'll be a whole new start. Out with the old, in with the new."

Gaia smiled slightly and looked up at Jake, who was already staring right at her. She felt a flutter in her heart as their eyes locked.

A whole new start, she thought. *Out with the old, in with the new.*

OLIVER SAT IN ONE OF THE FEW CHAIRS

Rejection

in his brownstone in Brooklyn, staring at the telephone on the table next to him. A half-empty bottle of scotch reflected the glow from the desk lamp that afforded the only light in the room. He took a swig of his drink and braced himself as the warm liquid burned down his throat.

It's just a phone call, he told himself. *You've taken phone calls from the president of the United States in your day. Just get it over with.*

He set the tumbler down, picked up the receiver, and quickly dialed Gaia and Tom's number. He had no idea why he was filled with such trepidation. Yes, there was a lot of bad history between him and his brother and niece, but that had all changed. They had fought side by side in Russia. They had escaped together. And even if he and Tom had been at each other's throats half the time, going through that experience together had brought them closer. He could feel it. Tom must have been feeling it too.

The phone rang a few times and he finally heard someone pick up at the other end. Oliver started to smile.

"Tom Moore," his brother said stiffly.

"Hello, Tom. How are you settling in?"

Silence. Oliver's heart thumped almost painfully.

"Tom?"

"I don't want you calling here again," his brother said, his tone impossibly cold.

"Tom. . . please, I just thought you and Gaia and I could get together," Oliver said, sitting forward in his seat. "Talk things over . . . maybe have a meal—"

"Until I know with absolute certainty that you had nothing to do with my kidnapping and with the threats to Gaia's life, I have nothing to say to you. And I don't want you contacting her," Tom said. "Do you understand me?"

Oliver struggled for words—a unique experience for him. Usually he could be smooth under any circumstances, could sweet-talk anyone and everyone he came into contact with. It was all part of his CIA training. But this . . . this flat out rejection from his only brother—his twin—was too much, even for him.

"Tom, I—"

"Stay away from my daughter, Oliver. Don't test me on this."

And with that, the line went dead. Oliver held the receiver against his face for a few moments, unable to move. He hadn't expected Tom to jump up and down and do cartwheels over the phone call, but this completely inhumane treatment was uncalled for. After everything he'd done to bring Tom home safely, everything he'd done to help his brother and his daughter, he certainly didn't deserve this.

Hand shaking, Oliver slowly lowered the receiver

onto the cradle. He took a steadying breath and lifted his drink again, downing the rest of it in one quick gulp.

It's going to be okay, he told himself, bracing his forearm with his other hand to stop the shaking. To stop the hot blood that coursed through his veins from pushing him toward the edge—toward anger. *He'll come around eventually.*

But his words were cold comfort to him, alone in his dark, unfurnished home. What did he have to do to get back in Tom's good graces? How many times would he have to prove himself?

To: Y
From: X22
Subject: Prisoner 352: Code name: Abel

    There has been a security breech in subsector K. Prisoner 352 is AWOL. Unconfirmed reports state that a young woman, believed to be Genesis, along with two men were instrumental in the liberation of 352/Abel. They are believed to be en route to the States, if not already there. We await your orders.